Paper Snowflakes

for

Christmas

PF Karlin

PF KARLIN PUBLISHING
SUGAR LAND, TEXAS

ISBN: 978-0-9890247-5-4

Paper Snowflakes for Christmas

By Karen Pugh…a.k.a. PF Karlin

Published by:
PF Karlin Publishing
Sugar Land, Texas

ISBN: 978-0-9890247-5-4
Printed and Published in the United States

ACKNOWLEDGEMENTS

I owe so much to my husband because I'd starve if not for his pizza making abilities. Also to friends, and fans for helping me muddle through to the completion of my third romance novel.

I'd like to give a shout out to the League of Romance Writers who's educational presentations have taught me everything I know about writing and for the Sprinting Groups that have help keep me on task.

A special thank you goes to Karen Sue Burns for plot inspirations, Kelly Larivee for reading the manuscript and her wonderful suggestions, Kadee McDonald for filling the role as contributor of things to try when things sometimes didn't work out, J.E. Martin who helped me fix those pesky page numbers, and Carol Mayer my editor who told me where I needed comas.

Last but and not least, many thanks to all of my readers, whose encouraging comments and reviews have been invaluable to me.

There are plans to expand the collection with several more novels in the Kismet Collection. The next will complete Belinda and Robert's story.

Watch for the third book of the Kismet Series:

Fulling Destiny

Paper Snowflakes

for

Christmas

CHAPTER 1

COLIN BROCKMAN FLIPPED on the switch to his new life.

The glass chandelier hung in the center of the great room and illuminated the large space. The light glittered to life as a starburst reflected in the polished wooden floors.

He laid four large suit bags across the massive marble kitchen island, careful to keep the designer pieces as wrinkle-free as possible. His suitcase hit the floor with a thud, and the sound resonated off the walls and the fifteen-foot ceilings.

Hand on hips, he surveyed the new dwelling and realized he needed his head examined for renting such a huge penthouse. But, that didn't matter. The high-end address was his ultimate goal to give the impression he'd made something of himself.

The bank of floor-to-ceiling windows that made up the far back wall of the great room beckoned him closer. One flick of his finger turned off the lights. The moon that hung in the night sky flooded the room with moonbeams. He waited for his night vision to adjust. Heel-to-toe steps echoed as he walked toward the outdoor scene of his apartment.

"Hmm. Nice"

He opened the solid pane double doors. The night spring air chilled his face. He walked to the edge of the balcony and grabbed the rail. The cold metal bit at his palms. There he scrutinized the view from twenty floors up. Against the black night sky, the lights from this cityscape in Toronto, Canada, were much different than his last home in Houston, Texas.

He inhaled then exhaled. This move marked a turning point in his life. The wealth-building strategy he laid out in college was about to become a reality. His promotion to vice-president kicked his investment potential up a notch, but once he made president, he'd be unstoppable.

"As beautiful as you are, I need to get busy." There was no time for scenery gazing. He checked his watch. Then he turned on his heels, flipped the light back on, and walked out the front door.

Fifteen minutes later, he returned with three boxes in tow on a hefty luggage cart, the total of all his worldly possessions. He slid the top one marked *kitchen* onto the island. The other two he dumped on the primary bedroom floor.

He zipped the blade of a pocket knife along the tape of the box marked *bedroom*. Then he pulled out a blow-up mattress and bed linens. After he inflated the mattress, he tossed sheets, a blanket, and two pillows with cases in a pile on the bed. He crossed his arms over his chest, rocked back on his heels, and let out a huff. The mattress occupied around ten percent of the floor space in the otherwise massive empty room.

He placed the other box on the double sink vanity of the primary bathroom and unpacked the entire bathroom in less than ten minutes.

Just before he turned off the light he caught a glimpse of himself in the mirror. *Are those dark circles forming*? He stepped back and turned his head from side to side. Only thirty-one, his age must be catching up to him if he couldn't handle a road trip like he did in his early twenties.

In the closet, he took his time unpacking the clothes that projected his outer shell. The ones that conveyed to the world he was successful.

In the top drawer of the built-in dresser, he placed and arranged a variety of silk ties to keep them pristine. Then he hung the professionally laundered shirts on a rod that ran the length of the closet. He lined his dress shoes on a bottom shelf like centennials keeping watch. The designer suits were hung on their padded hangers on the same rod as the shirts.

The feel of the fabrics screamed, "You made it." and he swore a cheap suit or dress shirt would never cover his body as long as he lived.

The rest of the stuff—shorts, t-shirts, socks, and underwear—were tossed in the remaining drawers.

When he finished he stood back and assessed the space. Out of all the rooms in the apartment, this was the most important. To him, the high-end clothes helped define who he was to the world. He had to admit, seeing the finished product gave him a sense of satisfaction.

The kitchen took no time and in less than an hour, he had unpacked his entire life.

At the entrance of the great room, he pointed to the right. "A few lawn chairs over there and a big screen TV above the fireplace. Yep. That's all I'll need."

He rubbed the back of his neck. Before his mother's summer visit, he'd make the place more presentable. A month's worth of rented furniture was enough to please his Mom. Once she left, everything could go back to normal.

He pulled out his phone to check for any calls or texts from the woman he loved with all his heart. Nothing. She was giving him space, but he owed his mom a, *I'm safe,* call.

"Hi, honey. I guess you're in your apartment? How is it?" Her buoyant voice lifted his mood.

"Nice. Big." He leaned against the cold marble island.

"How was the last leg of the drive?"

"Fine. I didn't stop to see much. Once I crossed into Canada. I figured we could do some of that when you come to visit. There's some nice tourist places not far."

"I'd like that. Are you all settled in?"

He let out a guttural laugh. "Are you trying to be funny?"

"Maybe. I bet it took you about an hour and a half."

He snorted. "You know me all too well. It took about an hour.

"Honey, why don't you think about furnishing the place this time since you plan on living there longer? You might be more comfortable with something that feels like a home."

"Mom. You know I'll make the place comfortable before you arrive.

Besides, I want to keep helping you with your rent, and now, I can get my investment plan going too. I can't waste money on useless crap."

"I wish you'd give it some thought. You might enjoy living in a place that has things you like and doesn't resemble a hotel except when I visit."

"I'm comfortable and have what I need."

He checked his watch. 9:30 p.m. If he rushed, he'd have enough time, and this was a good way to change the subject. "Mom, I have to go. I want to check out the office tonight."

"Okay. Now I can sleep well, knowing you're safe. I love you."

"I love you, too."

He studied his phone, his link to the woman who was this rock that grounded him, and the woman who molded him into the man he was today. After his father's death, she never remarried and raised him by herself. Somehow she always found a way.

❋❋❋

"Hi. My name is Colin Brockman. I'm the new vice-president of the Pendleton Financial Group. I'd like to go see the office." He pushed his name badge and passport across the counter toward the security guard sitting behind the desk.

The man furrowed his brow. "Kinda late, don't you think?"

"I just drove in from Houston. I'm officially starting work tomorrow, and I'd like to get a head start by figuring out the lay of the land."

The guard hesitated, then scooped up the badge and passport. He punched away at a keyboard, squinting at the screen. He held up the passport picture next to the screen and scanned back and forth from the computer to the passport, then to Colin. "Houston? As in Texas?"

"Yes, Sir."

"You say you drove."

"I did. I took my time and did some sightseeing on the way."

"Hmm. Long drive."

"Yes, it was." *What was so difficult about letting me into my office?* He flashed a Texas-size smile at the man. His secret weapon never failed.

The guard studied him. "Welcome to Canada, Sir. Use your badge for access to the last elevator on the left behind me. The Pendleton Group occupies the entire seventeenth floor. Your office is 1750. You'll find it in the back left corner."

The guard placed the badge in the passport and snapped it shut before handing it back. "Nice corner office with a view of the city."

"Thank you..." Colin strained to read the guard's badge. "John?"

"That's right. John Thornton."

"Nice to meet you, John. Are you a regular on this shift?"

"Yep."

"John, what time do you start?" Colin looked the man in the eye. He always made direct eye contact when he addressed anyone for the first time and repeated their names to help him remember.

"Around eleven and sometimes work the day shift."

"Well, John, I'm sure we'll be seeing more of each other. I tend to leave work around the time you arrive." Colin produced a smile and then turned to leave.

"Hold on, Sir." John opened a drawer and shuffled around pulling out a sealed envelope with Colin Brockman written on the front. "You'll need this to get into your office. It's the key. That's the only one."

"What happens if I lose it?" Colin flicked the envelope with his fingers.

"We change the lock."

Colin studied it. "Okay. Thanks, John. I'll be sure not to misplace this."

With badge, passport, and key in hand, he gave the man a salute and turned toward the elevators at the end of the lobby.

A pleasant elevator voice announced he had reached the seventeenth floor. He exited to a dimly lit reception area covered in mahogany paneling. Behind the reception desk, shiny backlit brass letters spelled out, The Pendleton Financial Group. To the left, a wall of windows framed the Toronto cityscape.

He shook his head. "Only, the best for Rob Pendleton."

The man who'd taken him under his wing, the man he owed his future to, and the only man who became the father he'd ever known.

Colin had a lot riding on the promotion. Most of all, he didn't want to fail and let Rob down. Heaviness hung in his heart at the mere thought of failure. Rob had placed his faith in him to complete a pivotal task that was crucial to the Pendleton Group. Colin was determined to prove he'd get the job done.

He turned around. To either side of the reception desk were halls. The logical choice was left since John explained the location of the V.P.'s office.

The hallway was long with doors of offices down the left side. The right was reserved for a copy room, public restrooms, and such.

The office doors on the left had brass plates with room numbers, names of the persons who occupied the office, and their titles. The long windows beside the doors with lights on gave him a glimpse into the offices and each occupant's taste in decor.

He stopped at a few windows to peek in as he progressed. A person's taste in clothes and objects they displayed around them told him a lot about that person. His business was reading people, and if he said so himself, he did an excellent job of trusting his instincts. More than once, a little voice in his head had led him down the right path.

As he made his way down the hall, he noticed the offices became larger and the titles of the occupants more prestigious.

He reached the last office before his. Jan Morin, Director of Marketing, 1749. He stopped to steal a look.

The vertical sliver of hall light reflected off a pair of creepy eyes staring back. He froze, and his heart jumped. Then he took a better look and decided to turn the knob. The door opened. *This shouldn't happen.*

He checked the name plate again. Yep. There in big letters was the word "Director," and all directors locked their doors, at least in the workplace that he managed.

He fumbled for the light switch. In the illuminated room, he laughed aloud. There, on an overstuffed wingback chair, sat a huge fuzzy teddy bear. Over the back of the chair was a woolen throw. The color of the throw matched the bear which gave the illusion the bear was bigger. Something about the teddy didn't fit.

The rest of the office appeared neat and tasteful. "I can't wait to meet Jan

Morin."

Curious about the unlocked door, he walked behind the desk. He tugged on a handle. The drawer didn't open. Relief washed over him. He tugged on another. Then he smiled. Her desk was locked down tighter than Fort Knox to keep the contents safe from prying eyes.

"Congratulations Jan, you just saved your ass." He turned off the light and closed the door.

As he walked to his next stop, his office, he took out his phone and spoke into the memo app. "Discuss security with my directors during their interviews."

In front of his door, he ran a finger over his name engraved on the door plate. He took a moment to let pride gush in before he opened the door, and then stepped into the outer office. Lit lamps on either side of a couch gave the space a cozy glow and behind the couch, more city scape views. "Fancy."

A desk sat to the right along the wall, facing into the room. He tapped the nameplate sitting front and center, Emma Ruddeford. "Hmm. My Executive Assistant, I presume. Can't wait to meet you."

He turned to scan the space. The only other door sat across from Ms. Ruddeford's desk. A little jump in his gut kicked. He never had a corner office. Correction, he never had an office and one this prestigious meant he'd leaped to a position of importance. He pointed. "And that's gotta be mine."

He slid the key in and turned. He pushed the door open a crack and then he stopped.

Movement from some place to the right side caused his heart to race. Maybe he should just back away and come back in the light of day. The teddy bear scared the crap out of him, but at least it didn't move. Whatever was in here was alive.

He pulled an umbrella from a cylindrical container next to the hall door and made a few practice stabs. "Not much, but you might help." He studied the tip as he walked back. "At least that's pointed and might do some damage."

With the umbrella held in a position to do bodily harm, he peered around the door's edge. If anything attacked, he positioned himself ready to slam the door if needed.

Moonlight spilled in over the seating area arranged in front of the windows.

He squinted, trying to figure out what he was seeing. A dainty arm flopped against the backrest of the couch.

What the...?

He rested the umbrella against the wall and walked in to find a woman sleeping. Long brown hair covered her face and obscured her features. She wore black yoga pants and a long-sleeved white t-shirt.

She moved.

A sudden jolt in his spine caused him to step back. The hairs on the back of his neck stood up and matched the pounding of the beat of his pulse.

She repositioned herself into a fetal position, wrapping her arms around her shoulders.

He took a few more steps back and glanced around the room. His little voice in his head screamed for him to get out of there. If a security guard making rounds found him in a dark office with a woman sleeping, his goals could end before they even started. One negative comment from the guard might send a flurry of rumors flying. He couldn't take a chance. Also, how would office gossip affect the woman on his couch?

He was sure she was breaking one or more company policies.

The reason she slept in his office, in an office with only one key that he had in his pocket, was a question to answer at another time.

He backed out and locked the door.

As he passed the Marketing Director's office, he stopped. Minutes later, he snuck back into his office to cover the sleeping woman with Jan Morin's borrowed throw.

"Sleep well, My Lady...whoever you are."

The elevator door opened after a ping. He waved as he passed the guard who raised his head just enough to peek over the desk.

John returned the gesture and asked, "Did you meet Emma?"

"Emma?" He stopped and hesitated, then made the connection. "My executive assistant? No. I didn't see her."

Was that Emma sleeping on my couch? He had no intention of saying anything until he had more information.

John punched in a few buttons on the keyboard. "Oh. She signed out. I must've been on rounds when she left. Nice lady and Mr. Tabor always spoke highly of her. I hear she's a hard worker."

"Well, thanks, and goodnight, John." Colin turned to walk out the door.

Maybe he didn't have a face for his sleeping beauty, but he had a name. And Emma had chalked up another infraction, clocking out without leaving the building.

Chapter 2

EMMA RUDDEFORD COVERED her face with the warm blanket that cradled her body. Her eyes popped wide. She peered at a bit of brown fabric wrapped over her head as the dappled sunlight filtered through.

I didn't have this when I fell asleep last night?

She shot to a sitting position. Her hair flew around until the brown tresses covered her face. She brushed them aside, then ran her hand down the soft throw. "Jan's. How in the ...?"

Her gaze darted around the office and froze on the briefcase next to her new boss's desk, that wasn't there the night before either.

"Crap." Her heartrate sprinted as she read 7:30 a.m. on her phone. Why did he come in so early? His welcome breakfast in the conference room didn't start until nine. She should know since she'd sent him the email invite, and he'd verified. The original plan was to be dressed and waiting with the rest of the staff in the conference room when he walked in.

She jumped up, angry with herself for sleeping so late and furious with her boss for being an early riser. She reached for the overnight bag she had stashed next to the couch. In full stride, she dashed toward the door. Before entering the outer office, she stuck her head out to make sure he wasn't around.

She adjusted her sights and headed toward the hall door.

The pounding in her chest reached new heights.

Cheek mushed against the window, she checked up and down the hall. No sign of anyone. A smudge remained on the glass. She pulled her sleeve over her hand and rubbed the smear, trying to make it disappear. All she did was make a bigger mess. The dirty window was the least of her problems. She had to get to the employee's restroom to make herself executive assistant ready.

This was not supposed to happen. Any other time, she'd use the private bathroom in the V.P.'s office to shower, clean up her mess, and get ready before anyone else came in. All anyone saw was her in the breakroom starting coffee or working at her desk. No one ever questioned when she'd arrived or if she even arrived.

Now, she'd have to use the employee's restroom and do a quick once over at the sink. The question was if she could make the distance between her office and the door down the hall without being seen.

Her new boss could fire her. What was she thinking? Could fire? He was going to fire her. She was fired.

Without reviewing the Policy and Procedure Manual, she knew of three violations that she'd broken. Sleeping in his office topped the list not to mention the use of an unauthorized key and clocking out illegally. Once he figured everything out, she was toast along with all her plans for independence.

The blood drained from her face. Losing her job meant continued homelessness and an indefinite delay in opening her retail shop. Something always pushed her plans back. First her divorce, now this. *How could I be so stupid*?

She peeked out and looked up and down the hall. The coast was clear. She made a dash for the restroom, pushed the door open, and then forced it shut. At least she'd be in an upright position and presentable when she met her new boss, who'd smash her life as his first official act as V.P.

Emma smacked her lips and wiped the corners of her mouth after she applied her favorite color of lipstick, *Fire Engine Red*, her only flashy make-up choice, actually her only flashy anything.

On the other side of the door, the muffled sounds of voices told her the office had come alive with coworkers. She stuffed her sleep wear and cosmetics back into her bag and walked out, heading for her office, prepared for the onslaught.

She secured the overnight bag into the bottom drawer of her desk. The inner office door was closed. Unlike her office, there was no window next to his. If he was in there that made no difference. She wasn't going to knock and find out.

A glance at the computer clock told her it was time to head out to meet the person who'd sealed her fate.

Why did he come in early and why didn't I have a place to sleep last night?

She watched as co-workers passed the window on their way to the conference room. "Well, time to meet my maker."

Hand on the knob, she took a deep breath and pulled.

"Well, good morning. Are you ready to meet the new boss?"

Emma jumped. Her hand flew across her mouth to muffle a squeak. "Georgia, you scared me half to death."

Georgia laughed. "Why?"

Emma waved her off. "I was thinking about something and didn't expect to see you right in my face."

"You're awful jumpy. How about hitting the bar tonight? We haven't had a girls' night out in a few weeks."

"I can't tonight. Maybe next week." She didn't even tell her best friend she had no roof over her head.

"Date. Well, are you ready?"

"For what?"

Georgia hooked her arm in hers and led her toward her doom. "The new boss? I hear he's a whole bunch of eye candy."

"Georgia, that's disrespectful."

"I can think whatever I want as long as you're the only one I tell out loud."

"Seriously?"

"Because you're my sister from another mother." She lifted her lids to glance at the ceiling. “To think of it, from another father, too.”

They shared a laugh and separated at the conference room door before they entered.

Emma scanned the room for a new face, and her heart almost stopped. At the far end, a man with sandy hair towered over the other occupants. The suit he wore fit his slender frame to a tee.

Georgia elbowed her. “That’s got to be him.”

“He certainly is tall.”

“And like I said, eye candy. Hi Asher.” Georgia waved to a broker standing against the far wall. “I’ll catch up with you later. My eye candy is standing over there.” As soon as the words left her mouth, she headed toward her newest love interest.

Alone, Emma tried to act as if she had a purpose for being there. Maybe standing in one spot to hold down the floor fit that need.

Soon the room filled with more people, and the decibels of the chatter increased. A few stopped to make small talk with her, but she made sure she positioned herself to keep the V.P. in her sights. After all, he walked in on her when she was at her most vulnerable and that embraced her.

He glanced at her. Her heart picked up speed. She wanted to run and protect herself from the big bad man at the other end of the room.

About to turn and make a speedy escape, her gaze drifted back once more to her boss, now busy hop-knobbing with several employees. She studied his near-perfect physique. Georgia was right. He was pleasant on the eyes. There was something about a man in a good suit that awoke sensations she hadn’t experienced in years.

Heck. What was she doing? That’s what attracted her to her husband, the bastard. Nope. She learned her lesson the hard way. Never again would she fall prey to a man with charm and money.

But the V.P. was very attractive and about her age. She shook her head. No. No. No. No. She needed to get those thoughts out of her brain right now. Besides, she had the company's “No Fraternization” policy on her side to keep her in check. She needed the job’s income more than a man in her life.

She filled her lungs and then exhaled, but the company's policies didn't stop her from breaking several rules these past two weeks. The reality of her current mess crept back into her head. She was screwed.

The former swarm of employees that surrounded the giant became less congested as they started to converge on the breakfast buffet. This was a good time for their second meeting. Except now she was awake. She took a step forward just as he planted his gaze on her. A half grin graced his face. His gaze fell on her chest.

What? Was he checking me out? You might be nice to look at Buddy, but you're crossing the line. Creep.

She glared back, trying to communicate her disapproval. She had nothing to lose, but he continued. Then he did something she didn't expect. He tapped his right index finger on his chest right over the center of his striped tie. Their gaze held. Then he did the tappy thing again and nodded his head down a smidge.

She studied him until she looked down to find she hadn't buttoned the top three buttons of her blouse. Heat rushed up her cheeks. Not only would he fire her for sleeping in his office, but she also made it worse by glaring at him.

This day just got worse.

One at a time, she buttoned her blouse and hoped no one else noticed her exposed bra which, in her book, was equal to a man's open fly.

With a glance back in the V. P.'s direction, she let out a sigh. Margaret Rice, the Director of Human Resources, slithered in and distracted him.

"May I have everyone's attention?" Margaret's nose shot into the air in her usual condescending way as she tapped her coffee cup. Silence fell over the conference room. She always demanded full attention whenever she went because she held the second-in-command position in the office.

Emma glanced around at her coworkers and watched the smiles vanish from their faces.

Margaret had a type of negativity that affected anyone around her. Not to mention that she scared most people to death. Ms. Personality she was not. The Witch of Human Resources latched onto the new V.P.'s arm and nestled in close. Almost too close to be appropriate. "I'd like to take this opportunity to welcome

Mr. Brockman to the company."

"Thank you, Ms. Rice." He patted her hand that clung to his arm and artfully released himself from her grip. Then he stepped to the side to address his employees.

Very slick and well done. His moves impressed Emma.

"It's a real pleasure to be here in Canada and to have this opportunity. I look forward to meeting all of you. So, if you get called into my office, don't worry the first visit will be a social one." His gaze fell on Emma.

Emma crossed her arms in front of her to keep her heart from jumping out. Was he giving her a signal?

They held the stare until Georgia popped into her field of vision. "He's done talking. Let's go get something to eat."

"What about Asher?"

"Yeah. Margaret's announcement kinda put a kibosh on my plans. He went over to talk to Mr. Brockman."

"Have you introduced yourself yet?"

"No. He's had people all around him." Emma flashed a glance in his direction. "See people everywhere."

"Hmm. I see Margaret is doing her thing." Georgia rested back on her heels. "I really don't like that woman."

"Georgia, she's your boss."

"So. I don't like her. She's not a nice person." Georgia nudged her arm. "You can meet him after Margaret slinks away. Let's go eat before everything is gone."

With her plate resting on the window sill, Emma watched Georgia flutter around like a butterfly. She moved from group to group until she talked to every person. The girl knew how to work a room.

Emma turned and gazed out the window, about to take a sip of coffee, when Georgia's voice caused her to stiffen and almost splash the drink on herself. She was a pile of nerves and Georgia wasn't helping.

"Well. Have you talked to him yet?"

The few people between her and her giant boss buffered her a little longer, but she had to introduce herself at some point. "No. Not yet."

"Why? I talked to him for about five minutes and he seems nice."

If Georgia knew the whole story, she'd understand why Emma wanted to avoid Colin Brockman for as long as possible. She glanced in his direction. "I'm sure he is. He's still pretty busy. Everyone in the room wants to talk to him."

"Except you. Go say hi. You'll have to, eventually. Remember, you sit in his outer office. No way to avoid him." Georgia raised both her brows and her eyes grew wide.

Georgia's words rattled her ears. "Give me just a sec."

"Okay. I'll come back and when I do, no excuses."

Emma turned back to the view out the window. *How did I get myself into this mess? Not only had I deceived Georgia, but I managed to get myself fired.*

Despite knowing Georgia since sixth grade, she hadn't confided in her best friend. She was too embarrassed to admit to her bestie that she had been right from the first day she met Benedict. Georgia told Emma to stay clear, but she didn't listen.

Georgia knew about the divorce and knew Emma would be dirt poor because of the prenup. However, Georgia didn't know that Emma considered herself homeless. On Saturday, four days from now, she'd sign a lease to her new apartment with the money she'd saved.

Last night wasn't the first time she'd camped out in the vacant office. She'd been sleeping there for the past month.

"Hi, Mr. Brockman. Let me introduce you to Emma, your Executive Assistant."

Emma's lids popped wide. Her skin prickled. Georgia's timing stunk, but this meant he was standing behind her. She wasn't ready to face him. Now, she had no choice. Her stomach clenched as she turned toward the giant.

"Welcome to the office." She hesitated before extending her hand. His glacier-blue eyes held her until Georgia broke the spell.

"Em, I see someone I need to talk to..." And Georgia was off, leaving her to fend for herself.

Colin shook her hand. "Hello. It's nice to meet you."

She forced a smile. Emma craned her neck to see his face because she came mid-chest to him. She guessed he had to be around six-four to her five-four. She figured he'd be polite in the conference room, but back in the privacy of his office, she'd be canned.

"Same here. What do you think so far?" She let her hand fall to her side.

"About what?" He regarded her with a half grin on his nicely featured face.

"Canada. Your employees. Your office."

He glanced around the room. "Canada. I don't know yet. I haven't seen much. The people, so far everyone has been really friendly. My office..." He rubbed his square jaw. "I was told the couch is comfortable."

Her stomach dropped seventeen floors. "Look, I'm sorry..."

He put up his hand. "Not here."

Chapter 3

EMMA'S MOUTH WENT dry as she watched the backside of a tall man with striking blue eyes in a perfectly tailored suit leave the room. Her shoulders went slack when air escaped her lungs. She followed several paces behind him.

She entered the outer office, which was empty, walked over to her boss's open door, and knocked.

"Mr. Brockman."

He was taking off his jacket and hanging it in the closet. "Please. Come in." He motioned for her to take a seat in front of his desk.

She sat, stiffened her back, and placed her folded hands on her lap. This reminded her of sitting in her soon-to-be ex-husband's lawyer's office. With no recourse in that situation, either.

He sat in the leather chair, nestled back, then leaned forward and rested his forearms on the desk with his fingers laced together.

This had to be his serious pose, the one where he tells her why he had to fire her.

"Can you tell me how to get a copy of the Policy and Procedure Manual?"

She blinked and the blood drained from her head. She wanted to puke but pulled it together to answer him. "It's on your computer."

His hands went in the air and then landed on either side of the keyboard. "I have no idea. Can you show me?"

Not only was he planning to fire her, but now he wanted her to help him do it. How could someone so good-looking be so cruel? She wasn't a mouse he could toss around to play with at his whim.

"Sure." She walked around and stood behind him. "Go to Documents. Now scroll down to Human Resources. Okay, scroll to Manuals. There it is."

She pointed to the screen and came to close to his shoulder. A whiff of leather and citrus scent excited her nose along with some of her inner parts. She stepped back.

"Well, that was easy. Thank you."

He turned to face her, and she fell under the spell of those eyes. Then he smiled and made the situation worse.

"Do you have time to talk?"

The blade of doom was about to drop. "I'm your assistant. My time is your time."

"Good. Please sit down."

She resumed her place in front of his desk. Glad to be far enough away so his scent no longer had an effect. Instead, her heart pounded a mile a minute in anticipation of what he said next.

He resumed his earlier position. "I'm not someone who... Let's see..." He focused on her face. "Beats around the bush. I'm direct."

And there it was. She sat staring into his baby blues, waiting for the, "I need to let you go," speech.

"Emma, I need to know I can trust you."

It took her a second to mentally grasp what he just said because of the surging butterflies that kept her insides swirling all morning. She came up with a good retort. "I was very loyal to Mr. Tabor."

"That's what I understand, but I need to know what is said in this office, stays in this office."

She nodded her head and knitted her brows. "Of course. That's a given, Sir."

He laughed. "Just Colin."

"Yes, Sir, Mr. Brockman." She wasn't going to give him or Margaret another reason to fire her. She'd already given him enough.

"I've been sent here to complete a specific task and I don't intend to fail. I can't talk about that right now, but you may hear things while I'm on the phone or talking to someone in the office. I need to know you won't repeat anything or gossip. I also need you to tell me the truth. No sugar coating anything if I ask." His face hardened. "Can you do that?"

What? Wait. What? This didn't sound like he planned to dismiss her, but was he kidding? She knew how to keep her mouth shut. "I've always done that."

He tapped his hands on the desk and rested back in his chair. "Now, tell me why I found you sleeping on my couch."

Oh, God. She had to cover her tracks. How could she tell him her next check would solve the temporary homeless problem? That her divorce wasn't even final and her husband had a mistress. She had to come up with something feasible because her private life was none of his business.

"I was getting the office ready for your arrival and finishing up paperwork. I told the security guard I'd be staying late. Around eight, I decided to just stretch out." She shrugged, telling him a half-truth and hoping she gave him enough. "I guess I fell asleep."

One side of his mouth jetted up and the sparkle she saw earlier in his glacier orbs returned. "So, is the couch comfortable?"

She couldn't help herself and a laugh escaped. "Yes, I'd say so. I was asleep in no time and didn't wake up until morning."

"You looked so comfortable I didn't want to wake you." He tapped his fingers. "I thought you might get cold during the night so I borrowed Jan's blanket. Can you get it back to her?"

"You came here last night?"

"I wanted to check out my office and found you..." He pointed to her temporary bed. "Right over there."

Oh crap. She just lied to him and did exactly what he asked her not to do. What if he knows more? "How long did you stay?"

"I left right after I covered you up." He pushed his head against the back of the chair and laughed. "Jan's darn teddy bear made my heart skip a few beats, but hearing something moving in my office almost gave me a heart attack."

"I'm sorry." He's acting like this is funny.

He laced his fingers behind his neck, sporting a full-blown smile. "I do like to work late. That might put a damper on your nap time." He winked.

Was she hearing right? It sounded like he wasn't firing her. At least not yet. She rubbed her hands on her thighs. "It won't happen again. Will there be anything else?"

"Not right now. Thank you." He turned to the computer screen. "Just make sure the blanket gets back to Jan and remember..." He waged a finger and raised a brow. "No more sugar coating."

She was sure he knew more than he let on, but she wasn't going to stir up that hornet's nest and chose to play dump. She picked up the throw and headed for the door.

"Wait."

Was this it? Did he have his fun and the time had come to ask her to call security and escort her out?

"Please, come back."

She did as he asked but stayed standing, clutching the soft throw in her hands. The feel of the soft fabric gave her some comfort.

"Why was I told I was the only one with a key to my office? A key I had to use to get in? Yet I found you in here."

She lowered her eyes. This time she'd tell the truth. "Mr. Tabor gave me the key. There were nights he asked me to clear his desk. I'd file his sensitive material and then lock up for him."

"When did you start doing that?"

"About a year ago." She raised her lids to watch his face. He regarded her, setting her nerves on edge.

"Did you ever read what he had on his desk?"

She swallowed hard. Of course, she did. Who wouldn't? She thought about saying no. but he asked her to tell the truth. She had nothing to lose except everything. "I did."

"I guess you know a lot about the workings of this company. Mr. Tabor must have trusted you."

"I do and he did."

"Get that back to Ms. Morin." He nodded toward the throw she'd held as he'd interrogated her.

"I'll get you the key."

"No. Keep it. You might need it in the future. But, please let security know there are now two keys. Tell them I found one in my desk."

"Alright." She turned to leave.

"Also tell them I gave one to you."

He's covering for me by giving me an excuse. "If you wish." She walked out confused over what just happened, but she got a pass and she still had a job.

Still mulling the conversation in her head, Emma knocked on Jan's open door.

Jan stopped typing on her computer and flashed a welcoming smile. "Emma. Come in."

She held the throw out in front of her. "I worked late last night and took a nap. I borrowed this. I hope you don't mind."

"I was wondering what happened to that. Just put it on the back of the chair."

"Who's this?" Emma rubbed the head of the huge teddy bear.

"My boyfriend bought the darn thing and brought it up here yesterday for our anniversary. We had dinner plans so I left him here."

Emma surveyed the door and the position of the chair. She bet those fixed glass spheres had a creepy glint and in the dark, even a grown man might get spooked.

"Well, I have to go. Happy anniversary." Emma inched toward the door. "New boss."

Back at her desk, the first task was to call Security to report the existence of the second key. Then she spent the rest of her day doing what she always did—answering the phone and being available for anything her boss needed. To say today was slow was an understatement. He never called once. He just tucked himself in his office with the door closed.

She dragged out her work for as long as possible, until six o'clock. Her desk was spotless. Every item on her to-do-list was finished, so she had no reason to stick around.

She knocked on Mr. Brockman's door before entering. "I'm getting ready to leave. Is there anything else I can do for you?"

He had taken off his tie and put his feet on his desk as he read through some documents. "No. Thank you. I'm fine. I'll see you tomorrow."

"Goodnight, Mr. Brockman."

"Colin." He gave a half-wave that ended their conversation.

"Right." Then she left.

To kill more time, Emma stopped to eat dinner and browse through the stacks of her favorite local bookstore. Then she drove the forty-five minutes to the house she once shared with her husband.

There she'd force herself to sleep in the farthest guest room from the primary. It was either that or her car. She couldn't afford to waste the money she needed for her new apartment on a hotel.

Bile rose in her throat. The thought of coming in close contact with her ex made her ill. She still had the right to come and go as she pleased, but he and his house turned her stomach.

Around 8:30 p.m., she pulled into the drive of the thirteen hundred and ninety-four square meter or fifteen thousand square foot mansion that she once called home. Lights showed through all the downstairs windows, and she saw movement in the kitchen.

She took a deep breath, then headed for the back and used her keys to open the mudroom door. Just before she entered the kitchen, she stopped to watch her husband's mistress dressed in one of his oversized T-shirts, moving around the kitchen as if she had lived there for years.

The woman stretched to reach a bowl on an upper shelf. The T-shirt slid up to just below her butt cheek. She gave up trying and called out, "Benedict, Darling, come in here. I need some help."

Emma froze but went unnoticed as her soon-to-be ex-husband walked in. He nuzzled the neck of his mistress and swung her around to face him. He lifted her to the island counter top and kissed her neck. His hands went for her legs as he pushed her knees apart and stepped between them.

Emma cleared her throat.

The mistress jumped.

Her ex glared. “What are you doing here?”

“I came to pick up a few of my things. Please don’t let me interfere.”

“You could’ve called.”

“What, and interrupt your fun? But wait—nothing I did ever stopped you.” She walked past the island into the dining room and over her shoulder muttered in a sarcastic tone, “Darling.”

The table was set for two with the china, silver, and crystal she had picked out before their wedding. Heat rushed to the top of her head. She picked up the pace through the formal living room.

“Where are you going?” Halfway up the stairs, he rushed toward her, grabbed her arm, and spun her around.

“Get your hand off of me.”

Pain throbbed under his grip. “Get your hand off of me!”

He squeezed harder.

The pain intensified. She wiggled to get out of his grasp. “Let me go.”

He gave one final squeeze then released her. “Where are you going?”

“I told you, to get some of my things.” She turned and started to walk up the stairs, the blood pounding in her ears. “Go back to whoever that is in the kitchen. I won’t be long.”

He came up behind her. “I want you out right now.”

She turned at the top of the stairs. “I have a right to be here. I might even stay and sleep in my bed.” The thought of staying the night in the bed he and his mistress had sex in made her cringe.

“You wouldn’t dare.”

She wanted to push him. To hurl him down the stairs, but that wasn’t her. She’d get her belongings and leave. She’d sleep in her car if necessary. “Benedict. I have a right to be here and to sleep here if I wish. Remember. It’s in the court order.”

“I don’t want you here.”

"Well too bad." She glared at him. She couldn't care less what he or his family thought of her. Soon she'd be free of the lot.

Without a word, she entered the bedroom. The bed was a mess. The sheets and pillows were thrown all over the floor. Thank heaven she didn't walk in on them. The vision in her head made her want to vomit. "Seems you had a good time."

"I did. Pig."

She stopped walking.

"Deborah does more for me than you ever could." He walked up behind her. "You're a pig and acted like one in bed. You disgust me."

Her respirations locked. His insults still stabbed hard. Tears threatened, but she'd die before she'd let him see her cry.

She walked into the bathroom. The counter was covered in things that didn't belong to her. In the closet, all her clothes were gone. "Where are my things?"

"In the garage. I packed them up to make room for Deborah's belongings."

She bolted out of the closet with fists clenched and stood inches from his face. "She's living here?"

"Yes, she is and there's not a thing you can do about that. Is there, Pig?"

"You got it all wrong. You're the pig and always have been." She pushed past and raced downstairs. "I'll get my boxes this weekend, Ass."

Deborah stood in the kitchen biting her thumb nail. She appeared to be about twenty to his thirty years. Yep, he was a pig. Emma commented as she passed, "I hope you know what you're getting into."

Emma slammed the door so hard she hoped she'd break the glass, but that didn't happen.

In the car, tears rolled down her cheeks followed by sobs. She buried her head in her arm across the steering wheel. Why she put up with his abuse for two years astounded her.

"Get your damn ass out of my driveway or I'll call the police."

Benedict ran toward the car. She started the engine and pulled out of the circular drive with no place to go.

CHAPTER 4

TEARS BLURRED EMMA'S vision and driving became difficult. She pulled over to wipe her wet lids and cheeks. Why did she ever believe he loved her?

Before the wedding, he manipulated her into signing a prenup. She was young, in love, and a fool for not reading the document. She loved him and never expected what happened right after their marriage.

She gripped the steering wheel.

Maybe she got what she deserved for being naive, but never again. No one would ever use her that way as long as she lived.

The dash clock read ten. She took a breath and started searching her phone for a cheap motel. Everything she could afford looked sleazy. She didn't need the Ritz, but clean and safe were the minimum standard.

She made a decision and started driving.

Thirty minutes later she parked in front of Georgia's apartment building. She walked to the back of the car and hauled out the suitcase she had stashed in the trunk. A rhythmic pound worked a path up to her ears and blocked out the street sounds around her.

Her suitcase full of clothes was her only link to a normal life. After work, she'd visit her car to unload the dirty clothes and switch them for clean ones. Her deception worked because she always looked like she started the day refreshed, despite never leaving the office. No one figured out the truth, not even Georgia.

In front of Georgia's door, her arms weighed heavy from her self-imposed guilt. She formed a fist to knock, then stopped and laid her open palm on the smooth surface.

How could she have failed so miserably by not telling Georgia about how Benedict tormented her for two years?

In college, he swept her off her feet. He was attentive and loving. After she signed the prenup and the honeymoon, he turned into Dr. Jekyll and Mr. Hyde. With the Hyde portion showing most of the time.

She rested her forehead on Georgia's door and relived his ridicule. Even in her head his words still cut deep and she'd never forget.

First, with little things. She didn't load the dishwasher the right way. His laundry wasn't folded to his satisfaction. Even in front of housekeeping staff, he'd complain about how inept she was because she couldn't manage the simplest things. He did his best to embarrass her whenever he had the chance. Then he'd go on a rant about how stupid she was.

Emma stepped away from the door. She watched her hands shake just like when Benedict backed her into a corner and screamed inches from her face, causing a knife-like pain in her ears. The only thing she could do then was stand there and shake as she pressed her palms to her ears.

Georgia knew he was scum and had warned her after the first time she met him. She always encouraged Emma to leave, but Emma hid the truth by making excuses. The more time went on, the easier hiding the truth became.

Two weeks earlier, she'd talked back to Benedict which was a big mistake, but how he reacted gave her the strength to leave.

She studied Georgia's door and shook her shaking hands. In the light of the apartment hallway, she closed her eyes and heard her lawyer's voice as clearly as she sat in his office months ago. "Go back and stay at the house."

She couldn't do that. She had to protect what little confidence and self-esteem she had left. Being homeless and camping out in an empty office was better, until tonight.

A sigh escaped and tears welled. *I did waste two years of my life on that ass.* Emma rubbed her trembling hand over the surface of her best friend's door.

The horror of her last night tormented her. Now, she'd have to come clean and tell Georgia everything.

It was getting late and if she didn't knock, she'd have to settle for whatever she'd find on the sheets of a cheap motel. Visions of a crime scene under a black light with luminal sprayed everywhere made her shiver.

Georgia's place was her only alternative, so she knocked.

"Hi." Georgia's sightline settled on the suitcase sitting on the floor. "Emma, what's going on?"

"Can I sleep on your couch?" Tears streamed down her cheeks.

Georgia raised a brow. She spread her arms and wrapped them around her. "Sweetie, of course, you can. I can even do one better. I have a very nice blowup mattress. Pick up that suitcase and get in here."

They walked into a comfortable, shabby chic, apartment Emma had helped Georgia design.

Georgia stroked her arm. "Would you like some tea before you tell me what's going on?"

"Do you have anything stronger?"

"Whiskey."

"Whiskey is good."

"Go sit on the couch."

Minutes later Georgia carried two shot glasses and a full bottle of Irish whiskey to the coffee table. She filled the glasses and handed one to Emma. The pair downed the shots.

"Alright, start talking."

"I left Benedict a month ago."

Georgia's eyes popped wide and a grin spread from ear to ear. "Now that deserves another round."

They swallowed the refilled glasses.

Emma gave her friend a recap of why she left Benedict. "He could've killed me when he threw a marble figurine. It flew right past my head and left a whole in the wall."

Emma's eyes filled with tears that made their way down her cheeks. "I ran upstairs and hid in a closet. When he fell asleep I packed a bag and left." She covered her face with her hands. Her chest heaved from the sobs.

"Come here." Georgia wrapped her arms around Emma. "We'll figure this out."

"I'm so embarrassed. You pegged him from the start."

"That doesn't matter now. What does matter is you're safe." Georgia stood and picked up a box of tissues from across the room. As she sat she handed a few to Emma.

"I couldn't live with him until the divorce was final, instead I started sleeping on the couch in the V.P.'s office."

Georgia knitted her brows. "Are you telling me you have not left the office in a month?"

"Yes. Other than making a trip to my car or getting something to eat." She sniffed. "Our new V.P. likes to work late and now I have no place to stay."

Georgia's mouth dropped open. With her dramatic flair, she used her hand to close it. She picked up the bottle and filled their glasses. She tossed her head back and drank away, then focused. "Why didn't you ask me if you could stay here the day you left your jerk of a husband?"

Her lower lip quivered. "I...I don't know."

"Oh. Don't start crying again or your eyes will be hell to fix with makeup in the morning. Here. Drink this down." She handed Emma her shot glass.

The second the glass was emptied she poured another. "The reason doesn't matter. Let's get you settled in. Afterward, we can have a few more of these while you fill me in on the details."

"This weekend I'll have enough for an apartment I found. I only need a few days."

"A few days or a few weeks, it doesn't matter. You can stay as long as you need. Grab that suitcase."

Emma followed her down the hall.

"Let's start with the bathroom. I keep a drawer empty for guests." She pulled some clean towels out of the hall closet. "You can hang these on the back of the door. I'll keep mine on the rods. Unpack your girly stuff in here and take a bath while I get your bed ready."

Georgia wrapped her arms around Emma's shoulders. "We've got this."

"Thanks."

"Take your time. I'm right out here if you need anything."

Emma glanced around the organized bathroom which was large for a one-bedroom apartment. She placed her suitcase on the counter and started to fill the drawer with her meager hygiene products.

Next, she ran a bath and indulged herself with some of Georgia's lavender bubble bath. The old claw-foot tub was deep, and she submerged herself in the warm water. This was heaven and the tension lodged in her muscles melted away. For the past two weeks, she lived under the constant fear of someone finding out about her homelessness. Surrounded by lavender-scented bubbles, a weight lifted. The fear she carried floated away on each bubble that touched her shin.

Why hadn't she asked her friend sooner? She knew the answer. She wanted to keep the one thing that she still owned, her pride.

Dressed in yoga pants and a t-shirt, she walked into the living room to find the couch moved in front of the bay window. The shades on all three windows were pulled down.

Georgia threw her hands in the air. "The room is a little smaller this way, but now you have some privacy." She pointed behind the couch.

Emma walked toward the windows to find an air mattress with cotton sheets and a flowered comforter tucked in the bay.

"You can store your folded clothes in the top two drawers of that." Georgia pointed to a dresser against the wall they thrifted and Emma painted. "I also made room in the hall closet for your hanging clothes, and if you need to wash anything, feel free. Washer and dryer are in the hall."

Emma released a heavy sigh. "Thank you for talking to your parents."

"What?"

"For taking me in."

"That happened in sixth grade. Why bring that up now?"

"Because, I wouldn't have had anyone, but now I have you and them."

Georgia fanned her face. "Now you're going to get me going. No tears.

Come here." She flung her arms around Emma and they embraced. Georgia took a sniff. "Ooh, lavender. My bubble bath?"

"Yep."

"Did you enjoy the soak?"

"I did."

"Good. Let's toss back another couple of shots. You got some 'splainin' to do."

Several hours and an empty bottle later, Emma slumped against the back of the couch. "So that's why I didn't ask you. I was too embarrassed."

"I won't say I told you so, but I told you so. I knew Benedict was dirt from the day I met him."

"I should've listened. I should've trusted your judgment."

Georgia waved her hands. "No. You were in love. Besides, should've, would've. What difference does that make? You left him and that's all that matters. When is the divorce final?"

"Since he's not protesting, in about a month. Maybe less." She looked at her friend. Tears welled. "How could I have been so stupid?"

Georgia held up a finger. "No tears. You don't want make-up issues in the morning." Then she wrapped her arm around Emma's shoulder and pulled her close. "Don't ever say that. You're not stupid. You just took a detour, but now you're back on track. Besides, you're the smartness I've ever known. "

"No, I'm not. This mess could set my plans back indefinitely."

"One step at a time. First, we get you set up in your apartment. You say adios to the jerk. Then you start saving everything you can to open your shop." She squeezed her. "Before you know it, you'll be your own boss. With no one telling you what to do."

"You know how much it will cost to furnish an apartment from scratch?"

Georgia pushed away and threw her hands in the air. "Look what we did here. I barely spent any money with our trash hauls and garage sale finds." She glanced around her living room. "I think we did good. When do you sign the lease?"

"This Saturday."

"Okay. I'll go with you bright and early. We'll hit garage sales before and after you sign the lease. You can take the air mattress and I'll lend you some kitchen stuff until we can get your place fixed up." Georgia bounced and clapped. "It's settled and it will be fun."

Emma took a deep breath. With a friend like her, she'd never be alone.

"Now I want to know what Eye Candy said after he found you on his couch."

"Hey. Show some respect."

"Why? I don't see that gorgeous hunk anywhere. Start talking."

Emma filled Georgia in on everything she could without breaking her promise to Mr. Brockman to keep the office business private. "He asked if I found the couch comfortable."

"What?"

Emma shrugged.

Georgia stopped and crossed her arms. "So he gave you a pass?"

"For now. Who knows, he might just be storing the information to use against me later."

"I hope not. He seems too nice to do that. I got a good vibe from him."

"I hope you're right, but now that gives him one more thing to hang over my head."

Georgia's brow rose. "Does the security guard know you were sleeping there?"

"John?" She gasped. "He knew I was working late. I told him there was a mess left after Mr. Tabor retired and I needed to clean things up before the new V.P. arrived. I made sure I locked the door and I never heard him try to come in.

"My point. You didn't hear Eye Candy either, and he was in the room while you were lying there, sacked out. Twice, may I add."

Emma's stomach twisted. "What if Mr. Brockman says something? You know how Margaret can be. She is so heartless. I'll be gone like that." She snapped her fingers.

"Or she'll boil you alive in her caldron." Georgia faked a stirring motion and let out a witch-type laugh. She sounded just like one.

"That's creepy." Emma huffed. "What if I have to forget about opening my shop?"

"Settle down. There's no need to go there yet. Just wait and see." Georgia patted her arm. "I have a feeling that Tall Drink of Water is tight-lipped. Remember, I have a good sense about these things."

"Now you have another name for him."

Georgia gave her a slight grin and shrugged. "Well, he did come from Texas."

"No respect." Emma checked the time, her head fuzzy from the shots. "It's one. We need to get some sleep."

They stood and Georgia gave her a big hug. "Really. You'll be alright. I'll keep my ear to the door and let you know if I hear any talk of firing."

"Okay." She swayed from the effects of the liquor as she held onto the edge of the couch to make her way to the air mattress. "Goodnight."

Halfway down the hall, Georgia shouted, "See you in the morning. I expect coffee by seven."

Emma stumbled to draw up a blind and then lay on her bed to gaze out the window at the stars above her head. The night sky was clear and each speck of light twinkled. Georgia was right. She'd get through this just like all the other trials she'd overcome in her life. Ending her marriage and hanging on to her job was no different. She'd learn from this and move on.

CHAPTER 5

EMMA WALKED TO her desk. The door to Mr. Brockman's office was closed. She took a deep breath and rubbed her forehead. Why did she let Georgia talk her into drinking so much? She sat at her desk, rested her head in her hands, and hoped her boss stayed in his office all day.

No such luck.

As if he read her mind, he opened the door. "Good morning." His voice boomed. She lifted her head just enough to acknowledge him.

"Hmm. Rough night?"

She sighed, placing her hands on the desk as she mustered what little energy she had left to sit straight. "Can I help you with something?"

"Yeah. I need access to all the employee personnel files. How do I do that?"

Great. That would involve permission from the Wicked Witch of Human Resources. Something she'd prefer to do when her head didn't hurt and she had all her wits. She didn't need to add dealing with Margaret to complicate her day. "Ms. Rice needs to allow that."

"She does? Even though I'm the vice-president I can't have free access?"

"Mr. Tabor told me to set things up that way to maintain employee confidentiality."

Something she never questioned if that kept her out of the path of Ms. Rice and she was sure Mr. Tabor felt the same. Margaret scared him to death.

"Can you get her to grant me access? I'd like that before noon."

"I'll get right on that, Mr. Brockman."

She dropped her head back into her hands. *Okay, now go away and let me suffer in peace.* No such luck.

"Emma, when no one is here, call me Colin."

"Yes, Sir."

Please leave me alone. He didn't. She met his gaze. He stood there and peered down at her then cocked a brow, and tilted his head. He was so cute. Puppy dog cute, but he needed to leave her alone.

She fixed on his eyes and sighed. "Yes, Sir. Colin."

"Better." He turned and went back to his office without closing the door.

Shit. They had a clear sightline of each other's desk with the door open and he made her situation worse. All she wanted to do was to lay her head down on her desk. With the door open, he took that option away. At least, if he stayed in his office, her minimal energy level might get her through the day.

She exhaled, but her relief was short-lived when she saw him starring at her.

"Emma please come in here."

She gripped her head. *Not so loud. Darn him. Can't he see I want to be left alone?* She stood and straightened before she approached the door. "Yes, Mr. Brock..."

His expression stopped her. "I don't see anyone else in here."

She couldn't win and didn't have the will to argue as she approached. "Colin."

On his desk sat a tray from the cafeteria with the remnants of his free breakfast, a nice benefit of his position.

"Have you taken any of these this morning?" He rattled a bottle of pills.

Even that made her head hurt. She squinted to read the label. "No, and I wouldn't touch your property."

"I know that. That's not what I'm asking. Have you taken anything for your hangover?"

He shook the bottle sending a wave of pain through her head Great. He figured out she drank too much the night before. What a way to keep impressing the man who held her job in his hands.

He shook the bottle again.

"Could you please stop doing that?"

"What?"

"The rattling." She made a shaking motion with her hand as she rubbed her forehead. "And no. I haven't."

"Oh. Sorry." He opened the bottle and shook two pills on a clean folded napkin that lay on the tray. "Here."

She picked them up.

"Wash them down with this." He handed her a glass of orange juice.

She eyed the glass.

"Don't worry, I didn't drink from it."

The pills slid down her throat with a gulp of O.J. as a chaser.

"Now, finish that." He pointed to the glass. "Trust me. It'll help."

She did as he asked and then placed the glass on the tray.

He walked around his desk and headed for the closet. "Okay. I've got a meeting and I'll be gone for about an hour and a half. I want you to lie down until you feel better." He motioned toward his couch. "You can use the blanket to cover up if you wish."

"Blanket?" Over the back of her frequent snoozing spot was a faux fur throw.

"I thought the office needed a little something. My attempt at decorating." He shoved his hands into his pockets. "Can't say I'm very good at it."

She scanned the office. No personal items had been placed anywhere. Not even a picture of his family. Everything was as bare as the previous owner, Mr. Tabor, left it after he sold the company and vacated the office.

"I think you need more than just that." She laughed. Her head throbbed. She pressed her hands on the sides of her head. "Oh. That hurts."

"Go on, get over there." He put on his jacket and headed for the door, then turned on his heels, walked to the credenza mini-frig, and pulled out two bottles of water. "Here. Drink these." He placed the bottles on the coffee table.

When he stood over her, he studied her sitting on the couch, and she studied him right back. “Now rest.”

She didn’t understand why he was being so nice. Other than Georgia and Georgia’s parents, no one ever cared how she felt or offered to take care of her. Yet this tall strange man appeared to care. His glacier blues penetrated her soul. Something inside stirred.

“I’ll lock the door on the way out and don’t worry about not being at your desk. As far as anyone is concerned, I have you running errands.” At the door, he hesitated. “That’s the story if anyone asks. Got it?”

She nodded, confused as heck.

“Now, lie down and rest.” The door closed and she heard the lock click.

Emma’s lids flickered open. She sat up and scanned the office. How long had she been out? The digital numbers on her phone told her forty-five minutes. She twisted off the cap of a bottle of water and drank, completing the promised two. With the headache gone, she felt more like her normal self.

She folded the throw and then placed it on a diagonal over the back of the couch. She gathered up the breakfast dishes to take to the break room. A cup of fresh coffee was next on her list.

From her desk she watched gray clouds gather. The weathermen forecasted spring showers for today. She didn’t care as she sniffed the aroma of her favorite beverage and closed her lids. The warmth on her hands spurred welcomed visions of winter. The best season of all because she could take to the ice. This year she’d have a pond to glide on right behind her new apartment. When ice skating, all her troubles always floated away, but she’d have at least nine months to wait for the pond to freeze over.

She glanced at the clock. Her boss requested access to personnel files before noon. She had two hours to manage the task. After the last swig of coffee, she headed for H.R., in better shape to take on the Wicked Witch.

“Hi, Roomie.”

Georgia's face lit up. “Why are you on this end of the seventeenth floor?”

"Col.." She flung a hand to her mouth. *Oh gosh. I almost slipped.*

"Are you calling Mr. Eye Candy by his first name?"

"No."

"Yeah. Right. If you say so." She gave Emma the once over with squinted lids. Georgia knew her too well and always knew when she lied.

"Why are you here?"

"Mr. Brockman needs access to the personnel files."

"Oh dear." She gave a glance at her boss's door. "At least you look like you feel better. I didn't think you'd make it out of the apartment this morning."

"I took something after I came in and drank some orange juice." What went on in the office stayed there even if Georgia was her Bestie. She'd made a promise. "Well."

A smirk covered Georgia's face. "I'll announce you, but you go in and ask. I stay out of that office as much as possible."

She picked up her hand set and punched a few numbers. They heard the phone in the inner office ring, and ring, and ring. Georgia's eyes rolled as she tapped a finger on the receiver until the ringing stopped. "Ms. Rice."

"What do you want?" roared over the phone.

Emma stiffened. This could be bad.

Georgia covered the mouth piece and mouthed, "See what I mean."

"Ms. Ruddeford is here with a request from Mr. Brockman. Should I send her in?"

After a pause, Margaret spoke, her voice softer. "By all means, please do."

Georgia and Emma looked at each other. Then Georgia turned a palm up toward the door. "Good luck."

Emma inched the door open. "Ms. Rice."

"Yes. Come in. What does Mr. Brockman need?" She stuck her nose in the air. Even when attempting to be nice, she still struck that condescending pose.

"He'd like access to all the personnel files before noon."

"Noon?" She slammed her fist on her desk.

Emma jumped. This woman has issues.

"That's not possible. I have to review everything before I just hand them to him. We have over thirty-five employees," she snarled.

Emma didn't understand why Margaret needed to inspect them. That seemed odd. "What would you like me to tell him?"

Margaret drummed her fingers and then gave the desk a quick tap. "Tell him I'll have some of the files to him before noon. Then I'll send another batch before three. The rest by five."

"Thank you. I'll let him know."

Something didn't sit right with the Witch's response, but it wasn't Emma's place to judge. She agreed with Georgia about staying out of that office as much as possible. She'd made the request, and she'd done her job.

When she arrived back at her desk, the inner office door was open and Colin was at his desk.

Emma knocked. "Mr. Brockman."

He shot her a cold stare.

She cleared her throat. "Colin."

He flashed a huge grin and motioned for her to enter. "Now was that so hard."

She sighed and walked in. "I went to see Ms. Rice."

"And, how do I access the files?"

Emma repeated what she'd been told.

Colin rested back in his chair. "Emma, what did Mr. Tabor do if he needed access?"

"He'd ask Ms. Rice for the files and she'd send them as a pdf. But only the ones he needed."

"Can anyone else access the files besides Ms. Rice?"

"No. Ms. Rice also said she'd have to review them before she sent them." She wanted to give her a real assessment of what Margaret intended but held her tongue.

He rubbed his jaw. A serious expression covered his face. Brows knitted, he didn't speak, like he was mulling something over. In a flash, he straightened. "Once we get all of them, would you be able to stay late if I need help?"

"I can manage that."

"I'll let you know. Until then this stays in this office."

"Of course."

Just before five, the last of the requested files arrived, pdfs of course, and she went in to tell Colin.

"How long do you think it will take you to separate everything into three files, employees with a clean record, employees who have warnings, and one for write-ups?"

"A couple of hours since everything is in pdf format. I'll have to read each file, but there shouldn't be that many in the last two categories."

"Then why didn't I get all these at one time?"

"I don't know."

Knowing Margaret she had to make sure she cleaned up her mess. Mr. Tabor never got involved with personnel issues. As a result, the old man lost some good employees at Margaret's hand. She knew how to cover her tracks, and if Emma had to bet, the records were immaculate and she only sent what she wanted him to see.

Emma's eyes stung from staring at the monitor for so long, but she was glad the remnants of her hangover were gone. She looked out the window. The rain passed and the sun started to set. In about an hour, the sky would darken.

As she suspected the files were perfect. Mrs. Clean worked her magic. However, more files than she expected had warnings for employees who worked hard and didn't normally cause problems. That number didn't seem right. She emailed the files to her boss.

"Colin," rolled off her tongue as she approached his desk. "I've got everything sorted and emailed to you."

He swung his head to face her with white teeth flashing and a sparkle in his blue eyes.

Her breathe hitched. After only one day, it became easy to use his first name. As Georgia said, he was nice and she trusted her bestie's instincts. Working for him just might be what she needed to get over her crazy marriage. He appeared easy going, considerate of others and not to mention good-looking.

"Well, Emma, I'm proud of you for using my first name."

Emma gave a slight curtsy.

He chuckled. “Anything out of the ordinary stick out?”

“Well. There’s a bunch of warnings on some employees I wouldn’t expect.”

“Let me look them over.” He seemed perplexed and appeared to drift off in his thoughts. He snapped back and focused on her. “How do you feel?”

“Fine.”

“And the headache?”

“Oh. That was gone after my nap. Thank you. Your remedies worked.”

“Tricks from my college years or I guess university depending on the country I’m in.”

She giggled.

“Did you get lunch?”

“No. I’ll grab something on the way home if you don’t need anything else.”

He stood. “Let me treat you to dinner. That’s the least I can do for you after all your help.”

“I think it’s the other way around. You helped me.”

“Okay. Then you treat me to dinner. Where should we go?”

Her mouth dropped open. Even a fast food place was too expensive for her budget. She didn’t have the money for a sit-down, and what kind of impression would a food truck leave?

“I...I...I...,” she stammered.

“I’m kidding.” He tilted his head. “Do you have a sweater or jacket?”

“No. Why would I need one?”

“You’ll see. Let’s go.” He picked up the throw on their way out.

She had called Georgia earlier to tell her she’d be late, and she’d take a bus home since Georgia drove. Dinner with her new boss wasn’t what she’d planned.

“I need to make a quick call. I’ll meet you by the elevator.”

The second he left, Emma called Georgia. She needed some level-headed advice.

“You’re going to dinner with him? Isn’t that fraternization?”

“Yeah. Oh, I don’t know. He wanted to thank me for working late. What was I going to say, no?”

"'No, thank you,' would work. You're treading in dangerous waters."

"Georgia, I'm not sleeping with the guy."

A pause came through the phone, and then Georgia blurted out words that caused Emma's cheeks to heat. "I could picture that."

"Georgia. Stop."

"Alright. Where are you going?"

"I have no idea, but stay by the phone in case I need a ride."

"My gut says he's not the type to try anything funny, but just be careful."

"Maybe. I gotta go. He's waiting. Stay by your phone."

CHAPTER 6

COLIN HELD THE elevator door open until Emma exited. She was a little thing to his six-foot-four frame and so cute. She had a nice figure, long chestnut hair, and eyes as inviting as pools of chocolate, his favorite desert.

From the second he saw her curled up on the couch, he fantasized about the mysterious woman he'd come to know as his executive assistant.

He knew his impromptu dinner invitation had the potential of entering into the realm of fraternization. That was the first policy he looked up after Emma helped him find the manual. He read he could admire her all he wanted, but couldn't touch. This adorable creature was off-limits as long as she worked in her current position.

"We go this way."

She followed until they arrived at his pride and joy. "Here she is." He stretched his arms as he stood alongside his Obsidian Black Mercedes.

"This is yours?"

"A beauty isn't she?" He rocked on his heels. Yeah. His little roaster screamed success.

"Did you buy the car since you moved here?"

"No. I drove her up from Texas."

She squinted. "What's her name?"

He scanned the car from bumper to bumper. "She doesn't have one. Have any ideas." He watched her place her hand near her mouth and rub one finger over her lips. Lips he'd love to taste. He couldn't keep his eyes off her. As long as he didn't touch, he'd be safe.

With slow small steps, she walked from the back to the front and then returned to his side. "How about 'Sadie'?"

"Hmmm. You think she looks like a Sadie."

"That's a southern name and she sure is sassy looking."

With a rub of his five o'clock shadow, he gave the name some consideration. "I like that. Sadie it is."

He approached Emma and placed the throw around her shoulders like a shawl. He held onto it which kept her close but not touching. Her lavender sent teased his nostrils. Their eyes met. If he tugged a little more, he'd reach her lips.

Was he out of his mind?

He released the edges of the throw and stepped back. "I'm putting the top down and don't want you to get cold."

"She blinked. "Okay."

He opened the passenger-side door and waited for her to slip in before he ran around to the driver's side.

She pointed her nose in the air and sniffed. "Sadie still has that new leather smell."

He took a whiff. "You're right." He retracted the roof. "Do you like seafood?"

"That's one of my favorites."

"Good. Rob told me about a place near the harbor. I thought we'd go there." One push of the ignition button and the engine hummed. A sound he'd never get used to.

"Is Rob one of your friends?"

He shook his head. "Rob Pendleton, the C.E.O."

"Oh. I thought his name was Robert."

"It is, but his son is also Robert so family we call the senior, Rob."

"Makes sense."

With his hand on the gearshift, he asked, "Ready?"

She nodded.

"Good. Let me show you what Sadie can do." He started to shift, then stopped. "I never named a car before." The corners of his mouth spread up into a grin. Emma had a playful side and he liked that.

He placed the car in reverse, backed out, shifted into first, and drove out of the parking lot.

As he predicted, there was a chill in the night air despite being mid-spring. He saw Emma tighten the throw around her with a smile across her face. She laid her head against the head rest and peered at the clear night.

"Well. What do you think?" He gave the car a little more gas.

Sadie accelerated and Emma stretched her arm to rest on the door where she let her hand ride the air waves. "This is...great."

"I thought you might enjoy it." Maybe he couldn't touch her, but he could show her who he was as a person. He liked to think he took care of the people who took care of him. His gut told him Emma fit into that category.

At some point, their situation could change. A promotion for her to a manager's position would solve the fraternization dilemma. Until then, he'd admire her all he wanted and keep a respectable distance. Right now, he needed her to help him meet his goal. Not to use her, but more like a colleague working toward the same thing. He had a strong sense she was not fond of Margaret which stacked the cards in his favor.

Form the reactions of the staff he observed how Margaret's negativity affected the office morale. Emma was no exception. Whenever Margaret entered a room, Emma tensed. On the outside, she remained calm, but her body language told a different story. Margaret caused an emotional reaction in Emma he didn't like. Maybe he couldn't physically comfort her, but he'd do his best to remove the person who caused her pain.

He pulled up to the front of the restaurant. After the roof clicked closed, she let the throw fall off her shoulders and reached for the door handle. He put his hand on her upper arm to stop her. Her muscles stiffen under his touch. Her respirations increased as she locked her gaze on his hand.

In his head, red flags went flying. Had she been mistreated? He released her.

"Sorry, but I'd like to get your door."

She jotted her chin out. "Do guys still do that?"

"This one does." Especially when he's trying to impress someone.

A few seconds later, he opened the passenger door and offered her his hand. She didn't move. *Did he spook her*? Then a dainty hand reached out and took his. She stood in front of him. Her respiration rate had slowed and she appeared more relaxed.

He made a mental note to be careful with his impulses to touch her. He had to make sure she controlled that aspect of this relationship, whatever their relationship turned into.

Their gazes met. "Thank you."

Behind her eyes, he saw a deep sadness, and a need to comfort her rose within. Right then he wanted to wrap his arms around her. To tell her everything was fine. But, that would be presumptuous on his part.

He had no right to invade her privacy and any action of that nature meant crossing the invisible fraternization line. He did the only thing he could do. He waved to the valet and handed over the keys. "Should we go in?"

He slipped the hostess a ten to seat them at a quite table were they could talk as he intended to find out more about her. Up to this point, he'd let his instincts guide him but she impressed him. "Would you like some wine with dinner?"

She peeked up from over her menu. Several blinks with her long lashes answered his question without her saying a word.

He poked a finger in the air. "Right. One rough night is bad. Two in a row is a killer."

"I'll have water."

After they ordered, the small talk started. Their conversation led into aspects about their earlier years to the present with nothing too life-riveting. He noticed she skirted around her family situation. He figured if she wanted to tell him she would and he was careful never to ask any questions that might stop the conversation.

He wanted to spend time with her and he'd let her disclose information about her past at her pace. He'd wait. Besides, there were things he could find out just by observation. Things like her quirky sense of humor. She even laughed at his lame jokes. *Where had she been all his life*?

Over dinner, he watched her every move. Graceful movements almost like a dancer. She let a hearty laugh when he attempted to be witty. Her eyes twinkled when she laughed. Her laughter was intoxicating. He wanted more of her, but he'd have to be patient.

Overall, he was glad he asked her to join him and from the way she relaxed, he suspected the same about her. However, he found himself getting interested in another untouchable woman. What did that say about him? He was nuts.

Emma checked her watch. "It's almost ten. I need to get going if you don't want me napping on your couch tomorrow."

"I might have to start charging you rent." He chuckled as he waved down the waiter and paid the bill.

They stood outside the restaurant, waiting for his car. "Where should I drop you?"

"I think there's a bus stop on the next block that will get me close to my place."

His mouth dropped open. "No way. You get dropped off at your front door. If something happened to you, who'd rent my couch? Not to mention I'd feel guilty as hell."

"I live about forty-five minutes away from here, one-way."

"That's fine. You saved me from eating alone. Driving you home is the least I can do." He guessed she saw the situation his way because she didn't protest, and that gave him forty-five more minutes to enjoy her company.

The drone of his car's engine grew louder as the valet pulled into the drive. Colin raised his brows. "Up or down?"

"Down. Definitely down."

"Well, get that throw wrapped around you," he said as he walked to the driver's side, leaving the valet to help her in.

The drive to her apartment was perfect. The route took them down the shore line of Lake Ontario until GPS had him turn to the west to travel the main roads to her place.

On her street, he pulled into the only parking spot he found about three-quarters down the block. When he came to a stop, he pushed the button to close the hood.

Emma darted her gaze up and around with an expression of shock. He even suspected he saw her stop breathing. She reached for the door handle.

“Thank you for dinner. I’ll see you in the morning.”

“Excuse me. What are you doing?” This time he kept his hands to himself.

“I’m getting out.”

“Remember. I open the door.”

She tsked. “I’m very capable of opening my door and walking home.”

He let out a sigh. “I know you’re capable of doing things for yourself. I just like treating my guests as though they are special. May I continue to do that for you and walk you to your door?”

Her eyes turned into saucers as her mouth parted a little. “Well. Okay.”

He got out and did what he said he’d do.

The chill lingered in the night air. “You might want to keep yourself wrapped up while we walk.”

She grabbed the throw from the front seat and placed it over her shoulders.

They didn’t say much as they walked. He didn’t know what to say or how to say that he found her captivating, that she was someone he’d love to get to know, that she was sexy as hell, and that he wanted to make love to her.

All his thoughts crossed the line. He’d have to rein them in until he promoted her to a management position and if she consented.

On her own, she had broken three company policies before he even knew who she was. As far as he knew, he was the only one in possession of that information. He had no intention of adding the fourth infraction of fraternization, and he wouldn’t be the one responsible for her dismissal.

At the outside door, she turned to face him, removed the throw, and handed it to him.

“Thank you. I had a nice time.”

“I did too. I’ll see you in the morning.”

She opened the outer door and went in. Partway up the stairs she turned and waved. He raised a hand and then she disappeared from his view.

Georgia sat on the couch and sprung at Emma like a cat as she walked in, grabbing her by the shoulders and giving her a shake. "Thank heaven you're here. I was going nuts. How was dinner? Did he try anything? Tell me. Please tell me."

"Georgia. Do you know how pathetic you sound right now?"

Georgia released her hold. "No, I don't."

"Let me change and I'll tell you all about it." She started down the hallway.

"I'll get the whiskey out."

Emma spun on her heels. "No. Axe the alcohol. I can't have a hangover two days in a row." Then she did a little jig. "But I'll tell you what he did for me before I came to see the Witch this afternoon."

Georgia gasped. "Go change and get back here fast. I want everything."

Emma brushed her hair and daydreamed about a tall, sandy-hair man who acted like a total gentleman, something she'd never experienced. He was old school when it came to manners.

She did a rerun of the entire day minus her trip to H.R. Everything about Colin made her wish she didn't work for him. If she didn't, they could see each other on a different level. Then again, their jobs brought them together.

"What's taking you so long?" Georgia's voice shrilled from the living room.

"I'll be right out. I'm almost finished."

She put a lid on her walk down memory lane and came back to reality. She wasn't even divorced and here she was fantasizing about her boss. She was nuts and needed her head examined. The idea of a relationship that would leave he incomeless was out of the question. She had plans for her future and wanted to stay on track.

"Hurry up!" A louder shriek came from beyond the bathroom door.

She sighed, put the brush down, and went to fill in her roommate.

Georgia settled in on the couch and grabbed a pillow to hug in front of her. "Start talking."

"He let me sleep off my hangover in his office."

"What?!" She clutched Emma's arm. "While he was in the office?"

"No, Silly. He left and told me to take a nap. He locked the door so no one could disturb me and even gave me an out if anyone wanted to know where I was."

"Wow. Then what?"

"We worked late and then he asked me to dinner." Emma continued to give Georgia everything she could that didn't pertain to office matters.

"He took you where? That has to be the most expensive seafood place in Toronto."

"I know. I was shocked. Then he opened doors, pulled out my chair, drove me home, and walked me to the door." Emma took a deep breath. "He treated me like a princess." She held up her finger. "We even named his new Mercedes."

Georgia shook her head. "What?"

"Before we left for dinner we stood by the car and gave her a name."

"And." Georgia made a circular motion with her hand to encourage Emma to continue.

"Sadie."

Georgia flopped back against the couch, still clutching the pillow. "Too bad you work for the guy, but this will make going to work interesting." She gave Emma's arm a shove. "It will give you something to look forward to."

"You're nuts."

"No. Think about how exciting this could be. You're both attracted to each other but can't make a move. It's forbidden love." She flung her hand to her forehead in a swoon. "This is the stuff romance novels are made of."

"Really? You've been reading too many of those." Yet Emma knew Georgia was right. Going to work every morning just became much more interesting.

CHAPTER 7

FOR THE REST of the week, Emma set up appointments for every Pendleton employee which started the following week on Monday. The "parade" would begin around ten in the morning, break for lunch, and continue until four. Each employee was given a time slot for a visit with Colin.

The final employee appointment, set two weeks away, was no other than the wonderful Margaret Rice. Emma saved the worst for last. Fortunately, Emma scheduled her for Monday which gave Colin the weekend to refuel and prepare for battle. He hadn't told her why he'd been sent to the Canadian branch, but she suspected the Director of H.R. had something to do with his mission.

Friday couldn't come soon enough, despite the thrill of seeing her handsome boss every day. She had a day of yard and garage sales planned with Georgia to look forward to on Saturday and a lease to sign that would solve her homeless problem.

"Emma, get up." Georgia rattled around in the kitchen on Saturday morning. Soon the aroma of brewing coffee filled the air.

That's all she needed to get her butt up and moving.

"We need to get going if we want to hit some good sales."

Emma shuffled into the kitchen after a quick bathroom visit. "What time is it?"

"Six?"

"Good grief. Why so early?" Came out through a yawn. She ran her fingers through her hair to get it out of her face.

"You don't want to miss all the good stuff."

"We don't even get up this early for work."

Georgia handed her a mug. "You can sleep as late as you want tomorrow. I promise I won't make any noise. Then in the afternoon, we go over to pick your clothes up from dipshit's garage and get you set up in the apartment."

"Which should take all of five minutes."

Georgia had just taken a mouthful of coffee. She turned toward the sink as the coffee sprayed out of her mouth and nose in the middle of a full laugh. "Look what you made me do."

"At least you were by the sink."

The two glanced at each other and busted out in laughter. Georgia swiped at her nose.

"Fix your coffee. I have to blow my nose and get ready." Georgia started to walk down the hall.

"I'll see what sales I can find near my apartment while I drink my coffee."

Georgia waved her hand above her head and swung her hips. "I'm one step ahead of you. I already did that. The Witch left early yesterday so I went down a rabbit hole. I've got a whole list and if we power shop, we should be able to hit about six to eight before the rental office opens.

"Okay. I'll make a list of things we need to find."

"Nope. I've done that too. I put both lists on my phone. Look them over while I get ready."

Emma nestled on the couch and hit the memo button on Georgia's phone. She only had about a hundred dollars to spend, but if they hit good sales, that translated into a bunch of stuff. She sipped her coffee as she studied the list.

"Okay, your next." Georgia came into the living room wrapping her auburn trusses up in a scrunchie.

"That didn't take long."

"Nope. We gotta hit the road. Get a move on."

"Stop being so bossy."

"Stop being so slow."

Emma grabbed some clothes out of the dresser and headed for the bathroom. She did the essentials and changed.

"Okay. I'm ready."

Georgia shoved an insulated cup of fresh coffee in her hands. "We'll use my car. It has more room. You're on navigation."

When the two of them decided to hit sales, they went beyond serious.

By the time the rental office opened, Emma had purchased enough kitchen items to open a small cooking school, which included a reproduction, eight-piece place setting of Delft dishes. They agreed not to purchase any furniture until after the contract was signed and Georgia had a chance to see the place.

Yard and garage sales were something they both enjoyed. With Emma starting from scratch, they'd have more Saturdays for their favorite sport. Money was tight so watching and waiting for a good sale was half the fun.

"Welcome to Pine Grove." The agent slid a copy of the signed contract and key across the desk.

"Thank you." With a stroke of a pen, Emma had a roof over her head.

"We completely cleaned and repainted the entire interior. Wait. Let me check something." She left and came back with a clipboard. "Yes. The carpeting was also changed in the bedrooms. The remaining hardwood floors had a professional cleaning. It should be move-in ready."

"Emma smiled. "Great and thank you again."

The girls walked to the car, picked up the sales finds, and carried their haul to the door of Apartment 110 which was at the back of the inner courtyard. Georgia adjusted the box she held. "This is nice."

Emma inserted the key. “You haven’t seen nothin’ yet.”

The smell of fresh paint hit her the second she opened the door. She stood in the living room and stopped.

“What’s wrong?”

She turned toward Georgia. “This is the first time I’ll be living alone.”

Georgia put down her box. “You’re right.” Then she laughed and slapped her on the shoulder “So, how does it feel to be an adult?”

“Not bad. I think I can get used to this.”

“Okay. I want to browse.” Georgia proceeded to move from room to room. She opened every door and cabinet of the two-bedroom apartment. “You did good, Emma. This is a nice place and in a decent neighborhood. Public transportation is close as well as stores and restaurants.” She walked past Emma and gave her a pat on the back. “Yep. You’re officially an adult, but why a two-bedroom?”

“I needed a workspace and a store room for all the items I plan to sell in my shop.”

“Makes sense. Can you afford this?”

“I plan on opening an online store to get things moving until I can swing a physical location.”

“Let me know. I’ll send my followers your way.”

“Thanks. But enough shop talk. You didn’t see the back patio.”

Georgia’s eyes shot wider. “Is it private?”

“Uh. Huh.” She positioned her friend in front of the close drapes in the dining area. “Ready?” With one pull of the cord, the drapes floated to the side to reveal the view beyond.

Georgia covered her mouth. “Oh, Em. Can you use it?”

She walked over and laced her arm into Georgia’s. “Yes I can. That was the first thing I asked.”

“For how long?”

“It’s not deep and I was told it can freeze as early as December and thaws maybe at the end of March if I’m lucky.”

“You did do good.” She reached over to wrap her hand around Emma’s as the two admired the small pond behind the apartment. They watched the late morning sun's rays bouncing over the ripples of Emma's future skating pond.

The pair decided to visit a few more sales to see if the sellers wanted to do any late afternoon bargaining.

"How much is this?" Emma studied the stone bowl she held.

"I can let it go for two dollars."

A grin spread across Emma's face as she dug in her pocket to hand over the money. "Here you go."

She joined Georgia picking through more kitchen items on a table. "What on earth is that?" Georgia took the bowl tucked under Emma's arm. "This doesn't look like something you'd put in your place." She studied the bowl more intensely. "It's to masculine."

Emma grabbed it back. "It's not for me. It's for Colin's coffee table in his office."

"First name and buying gifts for Mr. Eye Candy?"

"Stop it." She elbowed her bestie. "He insists on first names when it's just us. Besides, the office is so bare. He hasn't added anything except that throw across the couch. I don't think he's ever had an office to decorate."

Georgia held up the bowl. "The scale is right and it's dripping testosterone. Are you just going to tell him the office needs some work and hand it to him?"

"No. I think I'll just put it on the coffee table and see what happens."

Emma took the cold object from Georgia.

"And if he doesn't like it?"

Emma held it up to admire the sleek, clean lines. "Well, then I'll spray paint it and put some willow balls in it. I'll put it on that dinette table I just bought.

Georgia nodded and tugged at Emma's arm. "Keep me posted. Come on. It's getting late and I'm hungry."

Specks of sunlight dance across Emma's face through the maple tree outside Georgia's apartment. Emma stretched and turned to her side. She retrieved her phone, the display read 11:00 a.m. Georgia let Emma sleep in.

In the afternoon, the pair drove to Emma's last residence to retrieve her clothes, boxed and stored in the garage. The place was deserted when they arrived. She walked straight to the garage. As she suspected, he changed the code, but she had a key to the side door.

They entered the four-car garage.

"So where are they?" Georgia scanned the area.

Emma had a sick feeling. Benedict was a snake and she didn't put it passed him to donate everything. She whipped out her phone. "Where's my clothes?"

"How did you get into the garage?" Benedict protested in his condescending tone.

"Where's my clothes!"

"Gone."

"That wasn't part of the agreement."

"So what are you going to do about it?"

"Come home and find out. Maybe you should come right away and catch me emptying the place." She tried to bait him to find out where he was.

"I'm calling the police."

"Go ahead. I have the court order tin my hand to take my things and the decree doesn't specify what is mine. Consider anything I take as a trade for what you gave away and may I remind you, you broke the agreement first."

"How did I do that?"

"I have pictures of the bruise you left on my arm the other night. Do you want to fight about this? Fine, I'll be more than happy to take my share of your trust fund."

Her last remark shut him up. She almost heard those wheels in his head turn.

She could tell he wasn't driving and recognized some of his family member's voices in the background. When she heard his Dad yell at the TV she knew he was at his parents, at least five hours away.

She hedged her chances he wouldn't call the police. His trust fund was more important than fighting.

"You're an ass." She hung up.

Emma turned toward Georgia. "Stay here. I'll be right back. Get the back seat of your car down and back your car closer to the first garage door."

Emma stayed out of sight of the surveillance cameras and threw rocks to knock out the ones that covered the patio and garage area. She figured why give him a front-row seat of what she planned to remove. The patio French doors had key locks and like the garage, she still had a key.

The only obstacle left was the security code to disarm the house alarm. She punched in the last code. Go figure. It worked, lucky her. She pulled the alarm off the wall, disconnected the wires, and left it on the table. A wave of satisfaction coursed through her at the thought of him having to spend money to rewire the thing. *Score one for me.*

She raced back to the garage. She started pulling bins off of shelves and emptied the contents in the middle of the floor.

"What are you doing?" Georgia had a perplexed expression.

"Shopping." She shoved a bin at Georgia. "Fill this with tools. The kind of stuff I'd need to fix furniture. Make sure to grab that electric drill, sander, jigsaw, circular saw, and s bunch of hand tools. Once you're done, stack everything by the overhead door." She turned to leave. "Stuff them full. Then empty a few bins from this section and bring them into the kitchen."

Georgia's face beamed. "I'm on this. Anything to get back at the scum bag."

Emma wasted no time. She raced around the kitchen and selected items that would reduce her immediate financial outflow. Things like the K-cup coffee maker. She even threw in a bunch of loose K-cups, assorted flavors, of course. She grabbed anything she still needed to finish equipping her kitchen. A few higher-end gadgets, she had no use for, found their way onto the kitchen table. They'd be posted for sale online and their profits would ease her immediate cash problem.

Georgia walked through the door, empty bins in hand.

Emma held up a sauce pan. “Go get a flathead screwdriver and a few more bins” As she pulled more pots from the cabinet she placed them on the island.

Minutes later Georgia reappeared.

“Unscrew the handles and pack them. Then stuff the dish towels around them. Once you’re done, start to pack the stuff on the table. I’m going upstairs to get some linens.” She picked up two bins. “And maybe some curtains, blankets, and pillows.”

“How did you disable the alarm?”

Emma snickered. “The code worked. Benedict was always too confident. I guess he figured I wasn’t smart enough to do what we’re doing. Or fast enough to get into the house before he change the code remotely.”

Emma raced upstairs. There was limited space in Georgia’s SUV and she planned on filling every inch.

Emma stacked the full bins next to Georgia’s unexpected handy work on the floor. “What’s this?”

“Tables. I took the legs off so they’ll store flat.” She shook the screwdriver and then pointed it toward the tables. “I had to use this for something else and I figured you could use those.”

“Brilliant.”

They loaded the car to the roof, filling it to the max.

Georgia stepped back. “You know I bet we can tie those two barrel chairs from the living room on the top. They’d look nice in your apartment. I saw some traps in the garage and some nylon rope.”

Emma stood alongside her friend. “Good thinking.”

“And maybe a side table. We can stuff a few lamps next to the bins along the windows. You’ll have to hold the shades on your lap.”

“That’s not a problem.”

With her hands on her hips, Georgia studied the car. “I think this is more fun than garage sales. Can we come back in two weeks?”

Emma busted out laughing. She laughed so hard she bent at the waist and rested her hands on her knees until a pain hit her right flank. She grabbed her side. “This hurts.” But the sharp jab didn’t stop her from laughing more.

She stood up and rubbed her side. "You know, if we hurry, we could unload all this and come back for a second haul."

Georgia jumped and made a fast clapping motion.

"Let's go."

Once they shoved the last of their second haul into the back of Georgia's car, they drove off. Filled with determination, Emma had enough stuff to sell online that would push her budget ahead by several months.

After they unloaded the car, they spent the rest of the day unpacking. By seven, they sat on the dinette table eating pizza and drinking beer.

"So when do we hit the sales next?" Georgia took a huge bite and chewed away.

"If I stick to my budget, in two weeks, right after payday. We might want to find some resale shops and estate sales. I still need some of the bigger stuff." She paused. "Then again we could make another raid."

Georgia almost spit out the sip of beer she just took. "That was fun."

She covered Emma's hand. "You know, I'm proud of you for today. You stood up to him." Georgia took a swig of beer. "You'll have hours of stuff to talk over with your therapist."

A small piece of Emma's self-confidence made a path back into her soul. "I did, didn't I?"

"What are you going to do with this baby?" Georgia patted the top of the table.

"Chalk-paint for a distressed look and recover the seats in a rose floral fabric, of course." Laughter filled the air. Between Georgia and Colin, she started to laugh again, more than she had in the past two years. Laughing felt good.

After Georgia left, she walked around and imagined what she might do with her apartment. Her heart soared. She stood on the edge of hope for a new life and couldn't wait.

On Monday morning, Colin walked into the office. "Good morning."

Emma tapped away at her keyboard. “Good morning.” She held up a stack of envelopes. “Here’s your mail.”

He put down his briefcase and flipped throw the stack.

“It looks like a bunch of junk mail. If you’d like, I can shift through that and only give you the important ones,” Emma stated.

“I think I’d like that.” He placed a few junk envelopes on her desk. “Did you cancel the daily breakfast delivery?”

“I did.”

“I had to start going to the gym to work off the extra calories.”

Please stay fit. You’re so nice to look at. She got a grip. “Would you like some coffee? I can go get it.”

“I can go get it myself.”

“I know, but...” She rose and walked from behind her desk to stand next to him. Before she spoke she took a whiff to experience his cologne. She loved the scent. “I just like treating my boss as though he’s special. May I continue to do that for you and get your coffee?”

The shuffle of mail stopped. In a slow motion, a grin formed and he nodded his head. “Nice. Are you getting one for yourself?”

“I can. How do you like yours?”

“Well then, okay.” He turned toward his office door and gave her brief instructions on his coffee preferences.

He started his usual routine, about to place his briefcase on the empty coffee table before he hung up his suit jacket. Only the coffee table wasn’t empty. A sleek stone bowl sat in the middle with a note written on a paper snowflake. He walked around to study the details, and it fit perfectly in the space. He ripped off the note, *I hope you like this.*

Emma walked in with a mug in hand that had a swirl of steam circling above the rim. “Here. you go.”

“Thanks.” He pointed to the bowl. “Where did that come from?”

“I saw it and thought it would complement your new throw. So, I bought it.”

He placed his mug on the glass-topped coffee table and picked up the bowl. “This had to cost some money.”

He saw her drop her head. "Emma. How expensive was this? I need to pay you back."

"No. it's a gift."

"Thank you. Really. I appreciate the gesture, but I can't have you spending your hard-earned money on me. I need to pay you back." He put the bowl down and pulled out his wallet.

Her gaze stayed fixed on the floor.

"How much?"

She lifted her head enough to see him. "Two dollars."

He stopped counting his bills and glanced at the bowl. "That cost two whole dollars?"

"Yes."

"How?"

"I'm furnishing my new apartment. Georgie from H.R. and I are friends and we like to go to yard and garage sales on Saturday mornings. I found the bowl and thought that was the perfect place for it. So, I bought it." She adjusted her stance. "I guess it's a welcome to Canada and a thank-you gift for dinner all rolled into one."

He rubbed the back of his neck and scanned the office. The place didn't give the impression he wanted. The bare shelves screamed this guy needs help. If he tried his hand at decorating, he'd fill it with a bunch of tacky stuff. "Are you going to more of these sales soon?"

"In two weeks. After payday."

"If I gave you some money, would you buy some things that can make this office...more like me but with some taste?"

She let out a snort. "Are you telling me you have no taste in decorating?"

He threw up his arms and raised his brows. "I'd say so." Emma's cost-effective items could be the answer to his plain space problem and satisfy his need to save money.

She took a few steps and studied the room with her back to him. "Only if you let me photograph the space before and after I'm done."

"Why?"

She never turned around. "I have my reasons."

Who was he to pry? If she got the job done, that was a win-win, but he was sure he'd find out her secret in the future. "I can't see a problem with that."

"Maybe you'd like to join us and see if you can find your own treasures?" She turned her head over her shoulder, sporting a half-grin.

Emma just invited him to an activity away from the office. He needed to be careful. These were dangerous waters. He had to give his response some serious thought and take more time to answer wisely. Maybe give her an answer later in the day after he thought over the ramifications.

He opened his mouth to say *I'll think about it*, but instead, "I think I'd like that," tumbled out.

CHAPTER 8

ON TUESDAY MORNING, Colin walked behind his desk to find a neat stack of mail. Next to the pile was a cup of hot coffee, steam still rising over the rim. This morning a new item appeared, an empty picture frame.

An attached snowflake shape note read, *For someone important.*

He tapped the top of the frame. The only important someone in his life popped into mind, Emma. But placing her picture in the frame wasn't appropriate, at least not at the office.

The only other person that qualified as family was his mother. A picture of his mom on his desk didn't sit right with him. That shouted "Momma's Boy." Who he'd give the honor to, required some thought and lots of that.

Emma walked through the office door as he sat to open his mail.

"Your next appointment has arrived. Do you want to wait or start early?"

He pointed to the picture frame. "What's this?"

A slice of a grin formed. "Georgia couldn't use that so she asked me if I wanted it. I couldn't use it and thought it'd fit your office. Maybe for a picture of your parents or a girlfriend?"

Was she fishing? There wasn't time to tell her the story of his dad's death and that his mom was his only family left. "Did Georgia buy this at one of those sales?"

"I'm sure she did."

He gave a slight shake of his head. So, I'm second-hand three times over."

A small giggle escaped. "Yeah, I guess you are. Do you want it?

He picked up the frame and studied it. The quality was good and the style he could live with. "I'll keep it."

"So." Emma clasped her hands in front of her and shifted her weight. "Who's picture gets the honors?"

She was fishing. Her mannerisms made him smile and he almost forgot to answer her. "I'll have to think about it." He took a sip of coffee and adjusted mentally back into office mode. *Time to get the workday started and my mind off my adorable, Emma.* "Please, send in my appointment."

Over the next week, he spent time with each employee and discussed his visions for the financial group's growth with each. He also took the time to figure out which ones would remain loyal and which ones would leave. A leftover dilemma of any purchased company under new ownership and management.

By Friday afternoon, he had met every employee except for one. On Monday, he'd meet with the ripple in his calm sea that could cause a tsunami, Margaret Rice.

Despite his busy schedule, Colin's gut twisted every time he thought about spending time with Emma, on Saturday. He didn't know what was wrong with him because he hadn't had an infatuation this bad since high school.

By Friday he was a bundle of nerves. The next morning he'd be going out on his first-yard and garage sale adventure with his favorite assistant. The sale thing wasn't the important part. Spending time away from the office with Emma was. Georgia planned to come along and even if she didn't know it, she'd be Emma and his chaperone. Georgia's presence would remind him to watch himself around Emma.

He retrieved his meticulously hung jacket from the closet next to his restroom. He put the jacket on and adjusted his shirt collar. In his office a more relaxed attire was fine, but he wanted the world to see his polished side. Then he picked up his briefcase and headed straight to Emma's desk, keeping his cool. "So, what's the plan for tomorrow?"

Emma stopped typing and rested her cheek in her palm.

Her lashes fluttered and the jitters in his gut followed suit. Damn, she's adorable.

"Georgia's car is bigger than either of ours so she'll drive. Can you be at her place by six-thirty?"

"Six-thirty?"

"Yeah. We get coffee, drive to the first sale, then wait until they open. We move fast. You'll have to keep up."

"Give me her address."

She jotted the address on one of her snowflake notes and handed it to him.

The note made him smile and he fiddled with the tips. "Why snowflakes?"

"Snow means I can start to skate and it reminds me of Christmas."

He raised a brow.

"I love to ice skate and love the holidays."

"Oh." He placed the note in his pocket. "I'll see you at six-thirty and I'll bring the coffee." He turned to leave. "You like donuts?"

Her face lit up. "We love donuts."

"See you in the morning and go home."

As promised, he provided provisions. The three piled into Georgia's SUV and started hitting one sale after the other.

My eleven o'clock, he was tapped out. "Ladies, I'm no match for you. I think I need to quit." He swung his arm over the back seat to look over at their haul. "We did good. This was fun."

The women in the front glanced at each other. Emma explained, "We have two more to go. You can stay in the car if you're tired."

Georgia added, "Wimp."

"That's not fair. I just don't have my sale legs yet."

Georgia waved him off. "We should be the ones complaining. Your stride is two to our one."

He let out a grunt. At the next two stops, he stayed in the car, resting his eyes, and continued the practice on the ride back.

After they parked outside Georgia's apartment, Georgia grabbed her box out of the SUV and started walking away, then turned. She took slow steps backwards. "Hey, Colin. I had a good time. You goin' to join us in two weeks. That's our next time out."

"I'll have to get back to you about that." He wanted to see how Emma felt about him tagging along before he committed.

"If you do, I'll expect coffee and donuts. Em, we'll talk later." She punched the fob button that locked her car. "Once you close the back, she's locked." Then she walked up the outside steps and disappeared into the depths of the hallway just beyond the threshold.

He went to remove his office finds but Emma stopped him. "Let's put those in my car. There are a few changes I want to make."

He didn't question her and picked up their boxes.

"Is that everything?" Emma asked before she closed the hatch of the SUV.

He nodded and walked to the back of her car to load her trunk. "Thank you for inviting me. I enjoyed myself."

"I had fun too." She slammed the truck, walked to the driver's side, and slipped in. "I guess I'll see you on Monday."

Neither of them moved. He didn't know what she was waiting for but he didn't want her to leave. He didn't want the day to end. There was more they could do. Maybe go to dinner?

For a second a twinge sparked a glimmer of hope and he was about to ask...

She looked up. "Monday."

His spark turned into ash. "Monday."

He watched her drive away. One thing he was certain of, he didn't want to fall into the friend category again. He did that with Belinda and his emotions bounced all over the entire time. One friend-zone relationship was all he intended to have in his lifetime. How to move forward to a different level with Emma was the big question.

With Emma, what choice did he have? She needed her job and he had to do his to guarantee theirs.

From his pocket he pulled out her snowflake note. At least he held a little something that was once hers. He flicked the edge of one of the points.

Emma watched Colin standing in the street as she pulled away. A quiver in her chest gave her a warning she was falling for him. She could hear Georgia in her head. "Not again. You always pick the wrong guys. Getting involved with him will burn your plans. So, he's off limits."

Was that Georgia or her subconscious telling her what she knew in Georgia's voice? That didn't matter. The voice was right.

She carried Colin's box down the walkway toward her empty apartment. On the door was tapped a note. She unlocked the door and placed the box on the floor then pulled off the note. "What the heck?" Her presence was request in the apartment building's office.

A buzzer sounded when she entered. "Hi. I found this note tapped to my door. Apartment 110."

"Oh. I signed for a special delivery. This envelope was dropped off." The woman picked up a large brown envelop from the desk.

"Thank you." As Emma walked back to her place she tapped the exterior, trying to figure out what it might contain. She picked up her pace as curiosity took over.

She fumbled with her key which missed the mark a several times.

"Calm down." She took a deep breathe, then another. This time she managed to unlock the door.

In the privacy of her apartment she sat in one of the barrel chairs that graced the front of the picture window along with its mate. The side table sat in between with an expensive lamp on top, the result of her raid on Benedict. She broke open the seal. In her hand, she held legal papers that read her divorce was final.

She swallowed hard and then closed her eyes. For the first time in two years, she could relax. No longer did she have to endure his criticisms and harsh words. Words that made her feel less than others.

She was free.

Tears of joy flowed down her cheeks. In the dim light of the afternoon sun that dribbled through the sheer curtains, she became her own person.

She laughed. A dirt poor person, but giving up all the money was worth every penny. Clawing her way up was something she learned as a child and she'd do it again. This wasn't the first time and she doubted this would be the last time she'd have to start over. She had faith she'd manage.

She glanced around the apartment. One yard or garage sale at a time marked the start of her new journey by turning the apartment into a home.

Her first real home she had full control over.

At the same time, she'd save. Part-time, she'd get her online store pumping with the help of Georgia's social media presence. In a year, she'd open her life's dream, her shabby-chic retail shop.

Benedict never supported her dream. He'd made fun of her and put the idea down telling her she was stupid.

In some ways he was right. She was stupid for trying to please him. Every two weeks she'd turn her paycheck over for him to manage. He promised her the money belonged to her. He told her she'd have total access to the funds whenever she wanted. Then he'd make her beg until she gave up asking.

She shook the papers. "Stupid. Stupid. Stupid."

He stole her earnings and she let him. Her lawyer told her to fight for her paychecks, but she didn't have the energy and just wanted out. Her marriage was a low point in her life and her biggest regret.

Yet, the impromptu shopping spree at Benedict's place put her a few thousand dollars ahead and that lifted her sprits. After a quick swipe of her cheeks, she dug into her bag for her phone.

"Georgia, guess what."

"That beautiful boss of yours is at our apartment."

"What is wrong with you? No."

"I saw the two of you together. He's crushing on you."

No one spoke and of course, Georgia broke the silence. "Admit it you like him too."

Wait. What was happening? This wasn't the voice of reason I heard in her head when I left him in the street. This was all kinds of wrong, but Emma refused to take the bait right now. "Listen. My divorce is final. I got the papers."

"Well, that calls for an Irish Whiskey celebration. I'll be over in a few and I'll bring an overnight bag. I won't be able to drive home."

"No. I'll come over to your place and I'll bring a bag. Your place is more comfortable."

"But you have my air mattress."

"Yeah, and you have a couch and a bed. All I have is the air mattress and lots of floor space."

At nine o'clock sharp on Monday morning, his desk phone buzzed. He lifted the handset to hear Emma's voice which caused his heart to jump. He never wanted to take even the smallest moments with her for granted. "Yes."

"Ms. Rice is here," Emma announced.

At least she's punctual. He took a deep breath.

"Please send her in." He rose to wait for her arrival. He'd keep this meet and greet short because he didn't like the woman or what she was capable of.

After Rob Pendleton purchased the financial group, he came upon some disturbing information about his current Director of Human Resources. The last owner never dealt with the situation before he sold the company. Colin was sent to stop her.

"Mr. Brockman." Margaret approached with her hand outstretched.

"Thank you for coming to see me."

She took her hand and shook it.

After a reasonable handshake, he attempted to free himself, but she held tight. This was the second time she grabbed onto him and he didn't like that, but he remained composed.

"I'm glad you're allowing me to speak with you. I gather the employee files I sent were in order.

"Yes, all thirty-three were." *Except you didn't send yours.* "Please have a seat."

She let go when she was ready which told him she wanted control. She took a seat across from his desk. With her back stiff, she sat on the edge of the chair at an angle. Margaret crossed her ankles and her hands rested clasped on her lap. She must've taken lessons from some old Victorian etiquette book on how to sit. With her signature profile of her nose jetting into the air, she attempted a smile.

"This is an informal meeting and I'd just like to get to know a little more about you."

He'd been warned she was a fox and master manipulator. Rob got wind of her antics from a former employer with a different Canadian firm. One she sued for a substantial amount of money and won the court case. Her suit almost bankrupted that company.

That nose rose a centimeter more. "What would you like to know?"

The Pendleton Financial Group was sound, but paying her anything close to her last winnings would mean an end to the Canadian branch. They'd have to close the branch and layoff everyone including him.

The small talk started with questions about her childhood that led to her how she worked her way into her current position. Of course, she managed to eliminate the part about the law suit.

From what Rob had told him, he suspected anyone who got in her way ended up with a knife in their back and no job.

Colin needed to obtain and build a case against her so she had no recourse but to slink away into the night when she was asked to leave.

"Tell me, how do you like working for Mr. Pendleton so far?"

"Well, that all depends on what changes he has in mind and what direction he'd like to take the firm." Her nose rose higher and her high cheekbones intensified her slitted eyelids. "Doesn't it?"

"I guess you're right. I'll circle back on that in a few months." He glanced at the computer clock. Thirty minutes passed, more than enough time for him to get a better grasp on how to proceed with his hidden agenda.

"Thank you for coming in and I look forward to working with you." He stood but didn't extend his hand.

"And I the same." She turned to walk out.

As she approached the door he requested, "I'd like your employee file before the end of the day. You seemed to have forgotten to send it with the first request."

She stopped in mid-stride, never turned around, and nodded before she left.

He slouched in his chair and covered his mouth with his hand. How on earth was he going to build a concrete case?

He picked up the phone and called Rob. "I've got nothing so far. I reviewed the files and she scrubbed everything."

"I warned you she was a fox."

"There are several employees that have warnings in their files. Emma thinks there's more than usual. I don't know if Margaret followed protocol."

"See what you can find out but don't do anything to let Ms. Rice on."

"There are a few policies that give her too much power and I'll change those right away. However, I can't access the employee records without her permission."

"Well, that's not good."

Colin snorted. "I don't think the computers have been upgraded for years. All the departments are disconnected."

"I knew the system had to be integrated with the one in Houston when I bought Tabor's company and that would mean new equipment."

"Good because some of these computers are older than me."

A roar of laughter came over the phone. Rob was so loud Colin pulled the phone away from his ear.

"I'll have the I.T. guys we use here contact you to get your system upgraded and linked with ours, but here's how we'll do that." Their conversation lasted for twenty more minutes as Rob laid out his plan. "Don't tell anyone what you're up to. As far as they are concerned it's business as usual. We can handle all the details from this end. I don't want Margaret taking the opportunity to hide anything she might have stored as unauthorized files. Let's just let her think she's safe."

"Right."

CHAPTER 9

"IS IT DONE?"

"It is." Emma stood to follow Colin into his office.

After three months of sales, she'd cleaned, modified, and stored his finds in her workroom before they reached his office. This past Saturday, Georgia helped her move the items and put everything in place. She'd convinced him that making his dream come to fruition at one time had more of an impact than doing her job piece meal.

He walked to the middle of his office and put down his briefcase.

She held back to give him a chance to take in the room. She had to admit, this was some of her best work and he, her favorite client, inspired her creativity. Doing the design for him gave her a sense of accomplishment. Something she needed to make her feel good about herself.

A surge of butterflies sent her soaring over the memories of their secret get-togethers every other Saturday, sometimes with Georgia and sometimes not. The ones minus Georgia were the most enjoyable, but the most dangerous if anyone at the office found out. The finished space put an end to their Saturdays.

The office emitted a masculine vibe with expensive taste. The Persian rugs under the coffee table and chairs located in front of the desk completed the theme. The ceiling recessed lights caused a rainbow effect to filter through a crystal decanter and glasses placed on a metal tray in the middle of the credenza. The bookshelves behind his desk reflected his personality with one shelf dedicated to Mercedes roadsters.

"Emma, I can't tell you how much this means to me."

She bounced on her heels. "You're welcome."

"Did you get your pictures?"

"I took the before and after on Saturday."

When he turned, his smile caused her knees to wobble and a flutter erupted in the pit of her stomach.

His finger shot into the air. "I have something to show you." He picked up his briefcase, placed it on his desk, and then opened the lid. He took out the picture frame she had given him months before.

"I thought you had gotten rid of that."

"No. I just wasn't sure what picture to put in it."

"Who'd you give the privilege too?" She hoped to get more insight into his personal life.

"You'll see."

With the frame in hand, he approached the Mercedes shelf. He moved a few of the objects around to make space in the center where he placed the frame.

She was curious. She approached closer and stopped right behind him. She took a second and then stepped in for a closer look as she peeked around his arm. "You have got to be kidding me."

In the wood and silver frame was a picture of Colin with his arms crossed over his chest as he leaned against the wheel well of Sadie.

"So, what do you think?" He made a sudden turn to face her.

She didn't move fast enough and he clipped her jaw with his upper arm. She teetered and flayed her hands in the air, searching for something to give her support. She found Colin's shoulders.

He swung his other arm around her waist to catch her.

"Are you okay?" He rubbed his hand over her face and stopped to cup her cheek.

Their eyes met and just like that her heartbeat stretched on forever. A pounding thunder under her sternum prevented her from breathing. His scent of citrus and leather swirled and caused her head to do the same.

"I'm fine." He didn't release her from his grasp or gaze. With the back of his fingertips, he stroked her face.

"You sure? This might leave a mark. I can make an ice pack."

"I'm alright." She lied before she lowered her lids. She wanted him to pull her closer and encircle his arms around her. So she could take in his full scent not just a whiff. All she wanted was to press her lips to his.

He helped her steady before he let her go. He shoved his hands in his pockets as he took a few steps back. "You don't like my picture."

Was he serious? Her mind reeled from his closeness and he's asking her about a picture. She shook her head.

"What? That's perfect." He nudged his head toward the darn thing. "Do you know how much time I spent trying to get the picture just right?"

"Whatever." She turned and headed for the door. Their close physical contact continued to affect her. Not finding out what human he considered important disappointed her. Even though they spent hours over multiple Saturdays, he never spoke of family. She figured there wasn't a special someone because he didn't act like a man in a committed relationship or any relationship.

"Come on. Give me some credit here."

Almost to the door, she didn't turn around. "I'll be at my desk if you need me." She needed time to recover.

Emma concentrated on the computer screen to settle the butterflies when the outer door flew open and the Wicked Witch of H.R. stormed in. That was all she needed. The dose of Colin still had her on edge, now this.

Margaret planted her hands on Emma's desk. Her face twisted when she spoke, "What's the meaning of the policy changes?"

Emma didn't stand and Margaret didn't notice Colin's open door. Emma used a higher tone with the hopes Colin would hear. "You'll have to ask Mr. Brockman."

"I know you're the one who stated this by getting in his ear and talking about me. You're nothing but pond scum. You bottom feeder," She kept her voice low, but her face flushed.

Emma's hands started to shake. She dropped them on her lap out of view of Margaret as she grabbed her knees and squeezed. She hadn't shaken like that since the last time her ex screamed degrading insults and she was trapped with no place to run.

Just like now.

Colin's heart jumped and skipped around when he grabbed her waist. His impulse to kiss her heightened as he stroked her cheek.

Never again could he get that close. Arm's length—there had to be an arm's length between them at all times. Anything else meant trouble for him.

He kicked back in his chair with his arms crossed over his chest and scanned the office that Emma brought to life. He'd never bothered with making any space a reflection of himself. He liked the calming effect of the filled space that surrounded him.

Then he realized their standing every other Saturday date came to an end with the completion of his office. That he didn't like.

There had to be a way to keep spending time with her away from the office. He needed a reason, but what?

He drummed his fingers and then slowed the rhythmic beat to a stop. He had an empty apartment that needed to be furnished for his mother's visit in a few months. If he talked Emma into helping him, he'd be able to spend more time with her. He gave the desktop a quick slap. "Brilliant"

A muffled voice emerged from Emma's office. All he heard was his name and saw Margaret standing over Emma through the open door. The hairs on the back of his neck rose. He didn't like the view.

In the doorway, he motioned for Emma to stay seated. Emma dropped her trembling hands to her lap. What he heard made his blood boil. *Did she just call Emma a bottom feeder*?

That was it. No one in his office talks to anyone in that manner. Maybe he couldn't fire her over this, but she just gave him something he could use. He had grounds to give Margaret the first warning on her pristine employee record that took her two months to turn over after multiple requests.

Margaret leaned closer to Emma. "I can get you fired like this." she snapped her fingers inches from Emma's nose.

Emma jerked her head back.

"I've never liked you and you're...you're..."

Colin heard enough. "Well, Ms. Rice. What do I owe this visit to?"

Margaret stood and rubbed her hands down the front of her jacket that she buttoned at the waist and covered the top of the pencil skirt. She straitened her back and turned to face him. With contracted cheeks and vacant grey eyes, she forced a smile "Mr. Brockman, may I talk with you."

He stepped aside to allow her to pass then mouthed to Emma, "Are you okay."

She nodded.

He wasn't convinced. "Go take a break. Get out of here. Go for a walk outside and take your time."

She sighed and opened the bottom drawer, pulling out her bag. "I'll go to the coffee shop down the block."

"Good. Keep your phone handy and don't come back until I call you."

Margaret sat in a chair across from his desk, stiff as a board. Her head cocked toward the door.

With each step closer, his desire to lash out at her intensified. He had to control his temper because she just gave him an opportunity he needed.

He walked behind his desk, sat, and clasped his hands in front of him as he leaned in close. "Well, Ms. Rice, what can I do for you?"

"I'd like to discuss the policy changes."

"There's nothing to discuss."

She lifted that nose more, maybe a sign of her frustration.

"But I'm the Director of H.R. and I should have control of the employee records."

Colin loved this. He rested back in his chair and turned the corners of his mouth up. "And you still do with one exception, I'm your boss and I feel I have control over what takes place in this office. That includes access to everything."

The nose lowered and she dropped her mouth open.

He clasped his hands as he leaned over and rested his forearms on his desk. "Now I want to discuss what I just heard you call Ms. Ruddeford."

"What are you talking about?"

Was she going to play dumb? "Ms. Rice, I don't ever want to hear you or find out you have talked to an employee in that tone again. Do I make myself clear?"

"I have no idea what you're talking about. I was just asking some questions."

What did she take him for, an idiot? "That's not what I heard. I'm placing this as a warning on your record. I'll get this written up and send it for you to sign. If you don't sign it, that's your right, but it still goes in our file"

Her eyes grew larger the more he spoke.

"Is there anything else?"

She didn't respond.

"Thank you for coming in." He stood, hoping she'd take the hint.

She inhaled a deep breath, stood, and walked in short, fast steps out the door.

He just kicked his sleeping tiger. If he sat back and waited, she'd do his job for him. He needed to be ready and prepared for whatever she threw at him because that ripple in his calm sea just turned into a wave.

He glanced through his door to Emma's empty desk. In a flash, he called.

"Hey. Are you at the coffee shop?"

"Yes."

"Stay there. I'll come get you."

"No need."

"From what I saw, she upset you."

Silence.

"That wouldn't be the first time."

"She's talked like that to you before?" The back of his neck heated. "Did you report her?"

"To whom."

She had a point. Old man Tabor wanted to sell a company and made every working detail look pristine, even Margaret. "Wait for me. I'll be there soon."

"There's no need."

"Emma, please wait."

A sigh filled his ear. "Okay. Don't take too long and call if something changes."

"I will."

He gathered what he needed, opened his briefcase, and shoved everything in. Without thinking, he tugged his jacket off the hanger. About to step out into the hall, he stopped. He forgot to lock his door. The lock clicked.

"Jacket." He studied the fine fabric tossed over his arm which he always put on before he left his inner sanctum. He started for the outer door. "The hell with it."

Then the phone rang. There was no one there to answer his phone nor take messages. He glanced at his watch, two o'clock. He needed someone to answer the calls until five but had no idea how to forward them to anyone. Emma took care of details like that and he wasn't calling her to help him.

He's an adult and could figure this out. He just had to think.

"The receptionist, Sally."

He took a breath and walked into the hall then headed toward the front lobby.

Sally's chair was empty. Was she at lunch? Who answered calls when she wasn't around? He needed to pay more attention to these little details.

"What next?" He tapped the top level of the curved desk. "Georgia."

Her office was at the end of the right hall. He wasted no time and was never so glad to see Georgia's smiling face.

"Mr. Brockman."

He glanced at Margaret's door, which was closed. "Is she in there?"

"Nope. At lunch."

"Something came up and Emma had to leave early."

"Is everything alright?"

"She's fine." He understood how close the two were from their Saturday adventures. The pair told everything to each other.

"I have to leave and I hate to admit this, but I don't know how to transfer calls. I went to talk to Sally but I couldn't find her."

Georgia covered her mouth to hide a laugh. "Sally at lunch and I'm fielding calls. I can take care of yours as well."

"Great." He let out a breath of relief. "I'll see you in the morning."

"Tell Em to call me later."

He stopped at the door, tucked his chin, and turned to study Georgia. *Good heavens he didn't have time for this*. "Why do you think I'll see her?"

She offered no verbal explanation. She only smiled.

He waved a hand in defeat. "Yeah, I'll tell her."

Thirty minutes after his call to Emma, he walked into the coffee shop. He scanned every table until he saw her sitting in the back corner with her back to the door.

"Emma."

Her hands swiped her cheeks before she turned toward him.

His heart sank. How could he comfort her? If he touched her he wouldn't let go. He slipped into the seat across from hers. "I'm sorry she talked to you that way."

"It's not that. She just triggered some old memories."

"Would it help to talk about it?"

"No. I'm not ready. Maybe someday." She blotted her lower lids with a napkin. "I must look horrible."

"No not really." She was always beautiful to him. "Nothing a quick touch-up can't fix. Why not go do that and I'll wait."

She pursed her lips the walked to the restroom. About fifteen minutes later she returned. She clutched the strap of her bag and stood next to him. "I guess we should get back."

"Emma sit down." She did as he requested.

"We're done for today."

"What?"

"I'm giving us the rest of the day off."

"Why?"

"Because we both need it." He flattened his palms on the table. "Would you come to my apartment?"

Shock covered her face or maybe more like surprise. At least she asked for an explanation. "What for?" A tone of leeriness graced her question.

"I want to hire you."

She didn't respond. She just blinked her lashes in a way that melted his insides.

He paused. Yeah, he heard that. "Oh. That didn't come out right." He raised his hands. "Let me start over. I want to hire you to help me decorate my apartment. I figure if you saw it, you'd get an idea of what I need and..."

She shook her head. "Yes. I'll take a look, but what's this about hiring me?"

"I'd like to keep up the Saturday sales. I need the place fixed up before my mother's visit in the first part of September. We'll need to go out almost every Saturday. I don't think it's fair for you to give your time without getting paid."

She sat, thinking. "Okay. Let's go see your place before I give you an answer and we talk money."

CHAPTER 10

EVERY STEP ECHOED in the empty apartment as Emma walked around the island. She ran her fingers over the cool surface of the honed marble then walked into the great room and stood in front of the French doors. "How many bedrooms?"

Colin followed her. "Two. Guest bedroom on that side and primary over there." He pointed to his left.

"I assume two baths."

"That's right. There's also a half bath to the left of the front door."

She turned and walked to the guest room and then the guest bath. Both were a reasonable size. She pushed past Colin who stood in the doorway. "You said the primary is over here," her voice bounced off the walls as she walked between the island and the great room.

"Yes. Slow down."

"Why" Your legs are longer than mine. You have no excuse." In the primary, she halted. Her apartment would almost fit in this room alone.

Colin joined her at her side.

"How big is the apartment?"

He shrugged. "Two thousand square feet."

She pulled out her phone and tapped away. "One hundred eighty-six square meters." She moved her eyes from one side of the room to the other. "And your

Mom will be here the first week of September?"

"Yep."

"Where's your furniture? Did everything get lost when you moved?"

"You're looking at it." He spread his arms and made a full circle in the middle of the room.

"This looks almost like my place."

"This big?"

"No, this empty." She maneuvered around the air mattress and pointed. "I even sleep on one of those."

"And you're furniture is where?"

"Long story. I'll tell you some day." The real reason she shied away from the subject, she didn't want to start crying. The pain from her failed marriage started to diminish with Georgia's and her therapist's help. They were the only two who knew the complete story, for now.

"So. You want the job."

Yes, she wanted the job, but needed to get more details of what he expected. She was also interested in what he was willing to pay. The most important point, she wanted to make sure she won't get financially screwed over by another rich guy.

She sat on the edge of the mattress and rummaged through her bag. From the recesses, she pulled a twenty- five foot tape measurer and a small notebook. "Okay let's start to measure."

"You just happened to have a tape measurer."

She looked at the hunk of metal in her hand. "I never know when I'll need it. Like now. So yeah."

Within an hour, she had all the measurements and loaded her phone with pictures of every room at multiple angles. She shoved her supplies back into her purse.

"Now what?"

"You're taking me out to dinner."

He raised a brow. "Gladly. What are you in the mood for?"

She crossed her arms over her chest. "This is a work dinner. We have a bunch of planning to do and we need someplace quiet were we can sit and talk for a few hours. The food doesn't matter." She tugged at his shirt sleeve to get him moving.

He didn't protest but stopped in front of the island. "If you need a quiet place to talk and room to work, this is perfect." He placed a palm on the island. "Lighting's good."

"You have any food."

"Not really, but I do have this." He shook the phone in his hand. "And I can order anything you want."

That's right. Rich guys can buy anything they want, so why is this one so concerned about not spending money?

"I'll let you decide." She waved her hand over the space meant for chairs. "What do we sit on?"

"Those." He pointed to the lawn chairs in the living room. "They're high enough for the table height section of the island."

She walked over and dragged one to where they would work and tested it out. "I can deal with this."

"The pillows I added help make them higher."

"You've done this before."

He nodded his head.

She'd like to know with whom, but not her place to go there. "Do you have any paper that's bigger than my notebook?"

"Copy paper. It's on the back shelf in the primary closet. I'll order dinner while you get it."

When she opened the door to the walk-in closet, LED lights illuminated the massive space. On a top shelf in the back, she saw the paper. As she proceeded forward, she let her fingers float over the fine wool of his tailored suites that hung down the right side. She stopped to take a whiff and inhale his scent that lingered on one of the sleeves. His scent she'd never tire of. His dress shoes lined a lower self.

She poked her head out the door to make sure he was still on the phone. Then she opened the top drawer of one of the built-in dressers. Her mouth dropped open at the display of silk ties. He had filled the closet with expensive clothes, lived in a penthouse, and drove a Mercedes, yet he didn't have any furniture.

Something was wrong with this picture.

"Food will be here in twenty minutes."

"I'll be right out." She snatched up some of paper and rushed out of the closet.

"Good, you found it. Now what?"

"Now we start planning what you need to fill these rooms and how to do it. Sit down."

Until the doorbell rang they strategized.

"Ah. Food." Colin went to answer the door. He returned with several large white plastic bags that he placed on the upper level of the island. "Get your papers out of the way."

From one bag he pulled out two plastic place settings that resembled china. Form a cabinet by the sink he retrieved two wine glasses and a small candle in a glass container. Next, out came some flatware. He then set the table, lit the candle, and poured the wine. When he finished he made eating out of containers feel like fine dining. "Shall we start?"

Who was this guy? She took a second to study him before she sat, then wasted no time telling him her plan. "We're not going to find everything you need at sales. We might need to hit a few used furniture shops or estate sales."

"So you'll take the job."

"We haven't talked money yet."

"How does forty dollars an hour sound?"

Emma almost choked on her wine. She covered her mouth to cough. "Forty. That's too much." Although, that amount would give her a kick-start to solving her money problems.

"Okay, how about thirty."

She could live with that and not feel like she's taking advantage. "Okay."

"Good. But I reserve the right to pay a bonus. Agreed?"

"That sounds fair" She picked up her wine glass. "I guarantee your mother will be satisfied."

He smiled and clinked her glass. "Now all we need is a written agreement."

"What for?" She stopped and starred at him. She had signed one written agreement before and ended up in her mess called poverty.

"I want this to be strictly a business deal. I don't want any one from the office saying anything else. So far we've been lucky. I don't want that to run out."

"You mean Margaret."

He nodded.

That she understood.

"The agreement won't be all legalese. We can write it up and you'll have an equal say. He grabbed a blank piece of paper. "Let's start doing that right now."

The pair hashed out what Emma thought fair. "I'll type this up in the morning. Sally is a notary if you want to go that far."

"That might be a good idea. The word would get out but that might be something I can use."

Emma's suspicion rose. "Use?"

He spent the next thirty or so minutes divulging his plan to build a case against Margaret and explained why. "I wanted to wring her neck after hearing the way she talked to you, but I need more."

"Hmm. That might be tough if she's on to you."

"Maybe, but that's enough shop talk. Do we have an agreement?"

"Yep."

"It's getting late. Did you drive or did Georgia?"

"Georgia."

"Then I guess I better get you home."

She gathered up the papers.

At the open door, he waited until she walked into the hall. He pulled the door closed and paused until for the electronic lock to lock. "Oh, I forgot. Georgia wants you to call her."

Emma just smiled.

The next day, Colin walked into the conference room full of employees. After nearly four months of planning the time came to drop his bomb. At his side was, the Houston-based Information Technology department Director.

"I'd like to introduce Sam Matthews. He's here to help us upgrade our computer system so we can integrate it with the Houston system. Later this week, his team will start your training on how to use the new system."

Colin watched for Margaret's reaction. Her nose made the slow ascent and eye lids narrowed. Out of his four directors, she'd be the one he suspected of hiding unauthorized information.

Sam had been briefed by Rob about the situation and was on board about what to watch for.

"Today, he'll first start with the Director's computers and then his team will make their way through the complete office."

"Ms.Rice, your computer is first."

Her hand flew to her chest just below her throat. Did Colin detect some concern? He hoped so.

"Mr. Brockman."

"Yes, Ms. Rice."

"Could you start with one of the other directors?"

"I think it best Mr. Matthews starts with yours. The procedure has been well planned for several months to provide for an easy transition. I don't think changing the plan is a good idea. Please, show Mr. Matthews to your office."

Her nose rose higher. Her back stiffened. She rubbed her hands on her thighs. All her tells came out at once. Then she rose. "Follow me, Mr. Matthews."

At the door, she shot an icy share towards Colin with her grey eyes.

Colin prayed Sam would find something.

At the end of the day, Emma announced Sam wanted to see him.

"Send him in and ask him to close my door." He normally remained calm and level-headed in matters of business, but finding something he could use against Margaret kept his nerves unsettled all day. He found he had trouble concentrating on his work while waiting for Sam's report.

Colin stood to shake Sam's hand and directed him to the seating area. "Would you like something to drink?" He opened a mini-frig so Sam could see the selection. "Your choice."

"Water's fine."

"Need a glass?" Colin pointed to his crystal.

Sam grunted. "Nah. I might break it."

Colin handed the bottle to Sam who sat across from him, resting his forearms on his thighs. "Anything?"

"Nothing on the computer."

Colin gave out a loud sigh and bounced back into the chair. He tossed his hands into the air. "Now what."

Sam laughed.

"I don't think this is funny."

"Hold on. I said I didn't find anything on her computer, but I found this." He slid a flash drive toward him.

"She let you take this."

"Not without a protest. I told her it was against company policy to have unauthorized flash drives and that I'd need to look at the contents. I may have pushed it a bit too far because I told her if she didn't hand it over, I'd report her to the CEO."

Colin picked the drive up. "Have you looked at it?"

"Not yet." Sam stood and pointed his palm up toward Colin's desk. "Shall we."

"We shall."

After an hour of searching, they found nothing, but pictures of buildings and people in public places. The drive was a 2TB and it was loaded.

Sam tapped the mouse. "Colin this could take months for me to go through. From what Rob told me, she's pretty slick and could've hidden her files. If she knows how to encrypt them this will take longer." He huffed. "I'll have to take it back to Houston and see what I can do. I need to concentrate on converting the system right now."

Colin understood, but he was disappointed. He'd hoped the something would've stood out.

At a standstill, the system changes took place as scheduled over the next two weeks. One IT tech remained for the following month to help employees and make any tweaks.

Colin had his Saturdays with Emma to anticipate. They wrote and agreed on a contract with Sally as the notary. As he hopped the office came alive with speculations. Their agreement offered them protection against claims of fraternization. He made sure a copy was in their files and Rob was on board and copied.

The leaves started to change colors early. Colin was thrilled his mother would see as spectacular show of what his new home had to offer. Her plane was scheduled to land at six-thirty at Toronto Pearson International Airport. Colin was deep into some client accounts he wanted to finish before his week away from the office.

He glanced at his computer clock. “Emma, please come in here.”

“Okay. Give me a sec.” She continued to type on her computer, then she rose and walked into his office.

He held his car keys out. “I need some help. Can you take Sadie and go pick up my Mom?”

“Excuse me. You haven't seen your mother in over eight months and you want me to pick her up in your precious Sadie.” She crossed her arms. “What's wrong with that picture?”

He knew she was right but he had no choice. “If I don't get this work done before I leave, I won't be able to enjoy myself. Besides, I trust you with Mom and Sadie.” He lowered his lids and pushed out his lower lip. “Please.”

“Oh, stop it. Give me those.” She snatched the keys out of his hand.

He smiled and watched her melt. He loved the way his smile affected her. Over the past months, they formed a work-wife and work-husband relationship but always maintained boundaries that neither of them crossed.

CHAPTER 11

BEFORE EMMA LEFT, Colin called his mother to give her an update on the changed plans.

"I'll text you a picture of Emma and her telephone number. You know what Sadie looks like. Text Emma when you arrive. She'll be waiting in the cellphone lot."

"Okay, Sweetie. I gotta go. I'm getting ready to board."

"Love you. See you when you get here."

"Love you too."

His lips stretched from ear to ear. "My Mom and Sadie are in your hands."

Emma swallowed hard. "Gee, thanks. No pressure here."

Emma pushed start. The engine purred like she'd heard so many times on their weekends out, only this time she sat in the driver's seat. She gave Sadie a little gas. The car vibrated with power. She closed her eyes and prayed. "Please don't let me smash you up."

About fifteen minutes away from the airport, she received a text from Helen. The plane landed early and she'd be at passenger pick –up, waiting.

Emma's palms moistened. She rubbed them down her slacks. She'd be meeting his mother by herself. Butterflies swirled the closer she drove to the airport. *Why did I agree to this*?

She made her way to the United's International Flights passenger pick-up area. Traffic came to a halt with a sea of cars, luggage, and people trying their best to load up and leave.

At the far end of the sidewalk, she spotted a woman standing close to the curb. Could that be her? She made her way around the tangled mess of cars and then pulled into an open space.

Before she opened the door she reminded herself Helen was no different than anyone else. Who was she kidding? This was Colin's mother. She took a deep breath. It's now or never. With one push of the driver's side door, she popped out and flashed a broad smile. "Hi. Are you Helen?"

"Yes, I am and you must be Emma."

"In the flesh." Emma bent to pull the level that unlocked the trunk and walked around Sadie to help Helen with her luggage. "Let's get these back here."

When she opened the trunk, they stood shoulder to shoulder and stared.

Helen remarked, "They call that a trunk? I think my carry-on might fit in there, but nothing else."

"I agree." Emma leaned into the car on the passenger-side and pushed a button. The roof retracted. "The bigger one will fit back here." She went to lift the suitcase. Emma didn't consider herself a lightweight, but the thing was heavy. What did she pack for one week? She took a deep breath and bent her knees, ready to try again.

"Emma, let me help." Helen took hold of the handle at the top. "Grab the side handle and lift on three." Together they lifted and loaded.

Goal accomplished, Emma checked for damage to the car. Relief washed over her because Sadie survived. If anything had happened to Colin's precious baby, her promised bonus was history.

"Helen your chariot waits. I'll put the top up when I get in."

Helen smiled. "Can we keep it down?"

"Sure."

Close to the apartment Emma called Colin. "Are you home?"

"Yep. I just got here. How's Mom?"

"Good."

"The call's noisy. Is the top down?"

"Yes."

"Emma, I don't think that's a good idea."

"Mom's request."

He didn't respond right away. "I'll see you when I get here."

Emma punched in the code and opened Colin's apartment door.

The second Helen walked in Colin scooped her in his arms. "Mom, I missed you."

Emma watched them, feeling a stabbing pain grow around her heart. She never knew that kind of love from a parent. She had parents until the sixth grade, but she was more of an afterthought for them. Neither of her parents every hugged her like the embrace she witnessed between Colin and Helen.

"Is everyone hungry?" Colin waved his phone. "I'm taking orders."

After they decided what to eat, Helen walked into the living room. She wondered around with her mouth agape, touching various items.

The several table lamps gave the large room a cozy feel. An overstuffed sofa in front of the fireplace replaced Colin's lawn chairs. A large area rug muffled the sounds.

After a few minutes, Helen sat in one of the winged back chairs positioned in front of the doors to the balcony. "Emma, you helped him do this."

"Colin had the final say, but yes I helped."

Helen shook her head. "Thank you. Ever since he moved out, he's never made a proper home for himself. He's lived out of suitcases since he left."

"You're welcome. Would you like to see your room?"

Helen's face lit up. "I would."

Emma rolled Helen's suitcase into the quest bedroom. The walls sported a new coat of pale peach paint. A floral cream, teal, and peach comforter covered the queen bed. Matching curtains and pillow shams completed the effect.

"Colin wanted this room to be more feminine for you."

"It's perfect." Helen clasped her hands in front of her a she studied the room. She scanned every inch. "The artwork, chair and that throw are perfect."

Beaming from ear to ear she grabbed Emma's hand. "Now, let's go see his bedroom." They rushed past Colin who just finished ordering.

Helen covered her mouth when they entered the room. "This is beautiful."

A four-poster bed sat on the feature wall. Bookshelves lined the wall opposite the wall-to-ceiling windows. In front of the fire place, across from the bed, was a seating area with a couch and two chairs. Tables, lamps, rugs, and whatnots completed the room, all done with a classic traditional touch.

"She did a good job, didn't she?" Colin placed his arm around Emma and tugged her to his side. "And none of this is rented."

Emma laughed and placed a hand on his chest as she peered up at him. His warmth made her feel safe and she liked his closeness. She did nothing to discourage his show of affection. "You helped even though you had a hard time making decisions."

Just then the doorbell rang.

"That should be the food." Colin released her.

Their bond broke and the air chilled in the space where Colin had stood. Emma lingered, she had to remember he was her boss and she needed to stop acting like a love-sick puppy.

Colin parked the car and opened the passenger door like he'd done a hundred times before. He'd never tire of walking her to her door. A few times they came close to kissing. Inches from her lips, he always managed to step back. Then he'd remind himself that they had a business arrangement until the day he could offer her Margaret's management position.

He leaned against the wall next to her door. "I think you'll be getting a bonus. Mom seemed pretty pleased."

"I'm glad. I like her."

"I think the feeling's mutual by the way you two talked over dinner."

"I hope so. I better go in. One of us has to work in the morning." She stood with her hand on the knob but didn't leave. "Have fun during your week off. Try to relax."

He remained resting against the wall.

"What are you waiting for?"

"For you to walk into your apartment and lock your door."

"Colin, I'm fine."

He shook his head. "Nope. Sorry. Bro code. I have to know you're in that apartment. Safe."

She let out a sigh and dropped her hands against her thighs. "Okay. Goodnight."

He waited to hear the lock click before he walked back to the car. For a whole week, he'd have to endure not seeing her radiant face. Could he survive?

Monday morning Emma entered her office with two cups of coffee after a routine stop at the breakroom. She stopped mid-stride in the center of her office and closed her eyes. "What am I doing? He's not here."

She laughed at herself then noticed an envelope taped to her monitor. Her name was written across the front in Colin's handwriting. "When did he do this?"

Inside she found a snowflake made from a piece of copy paper. She unfolded the handmade note and read:

Thank you for the enjoyable Saturdays and all your help with the apartment. Here's your bonus. Skating is around the corner.

Below the message, he drew a stick figure ice skater. A surge of blood rushed to her heart and caused her pulse to speed up. "Ah. How sweet."

Then she saw the amount on the check. If her heart was racing from his note, what she read made it to hammer.

The check was for $4,000.00. When she added that to what he already paid, the total came to almost $9,000.00. In the memo area of the check read, Bonus for Decorating Consultant & Not Too Much!

Air refused to exit her lungs. She stared at the check. The bonus plus what she managed to make with her online store bumped her savings to $20,000.00. Emma's Attic was coming closer to becoming a reality.

The rest of the day was boring, but she had his note to read and reread to past the time.

Tuesday was a different story. Emma hadn't even reached her desk when Georgia burst in. "Did you hear?"

"Hear what?"

Georgia grabbed Emma by the shoulders. "Margaret fired Keith yesterday." She darted her gaze over her shoulder. "And I'll be next if she sees me in here."

Emma dug her keys out of her purse. "Come on. We can talk in here."

She opened the door to Colin's office and motioned for her to sit on the couch. Then closed and locked the door behind her. Since Colin was gone and she had the only other key. Not even the Wicked Witch could get to them. They were safe. "Tell me what happened."

"No one knows. She called him into her office late yesterday. Everyone else was gone. I heard from security guard that she asked him to escort Keith out."

Emma concentrated on Georgia. "There has to be something in his record as to why. She can't just fire employees because she wants to." Emma stood and walked over to Colin's computer. She typed in his password.

Georgia hovered over her shoulder. "You know his password?"

"Quite." She ran a search of the employee records to find Keith's file missing. "It's not here?"

Georgia leaned in closer. "It has to be."

"Nope. She wiped it." The two looked at each other.

Georgia stood. "You need to call Colin."

"No. I'm going to let her do whatever she has planned. When Colin gets back, he'll fix this." Emma pushed away from the desk. "Besides, he needs the time off to visit with his mom."

"I got to get back before she notices I've been gone. I'll stay I high alert to see if I can find out anything else."

On Wednesday, Sally was terminated and as with Keith, her records went missing.

Loosing those two vital employees threw the office into turmoil.

Emma's phone rang. "Mr. Brockman's office. May I help you?"

"Em, get down here right away." Georgia's voice sounded panicked. Something out of character for her.

"What's wrong."

"She wants us in here office. Em, I'm scared. I need this job."

Emma's stomach clenched. "If she tries firing us, I'll call Colin. I'll be right down."

Emma's neck heated and she clenched her fists. She stood and walked down to the Witch's office prepared for battle.

Georgia's face screamed fear. "I'll let her know you're here."

After Georgia informed Margaret. They walked into her office and sat down.

"There's been a few personnel changes in the past two days which will mean more work for the two of you. Besides your regular duties, you'll be expected to handle several others."

Margaret reviewed a list that included sending letters to Keith's clients, follow-up phone calls, taking turns working the reception desk, and manning the incoming calls. "Not," She stated. "A complete list."

"But our work load will double," Emma pointed out.

Margaret acted bored. "And?"

"We'll be working ten hours a day," Georgia chimed in.

"Without overtime." She glared. "Do I make myself clear?"

"Yes," they answered simultaneously.

"Alright. Go. Leave the door open."

They couldn't talk right then but Emma knew Georgia well enough that a bathroom break was about to take place in Colin's office.

Emma rushed back and unlocked Colin's door. She didn't want to waste any of Georgia's precious time. They'd have to talk fast.

As predicted Georgia pushed the outer office door with force. She clenched her fist. “She’s just stirring up shit to make everyone’s life miserable.”

“Not out here.” Emma pointed to the safety of the inner office.

Georgia followed Emma.

Margaret won with her mini-coup but there was no reason to call Colin with two days left in the week. They’d hold down the fort until he returned.

CHAPTER 12

EMMA NEVER CALLED Colin. On Monday morning he returned to find Emma sitting at the reception desk managing incoming calls and appointments.

"What are you doing out here?"

"I have so much to tell you. Let me get Georgia to cover. I'll meet you in the office."

Emma continued to man the phones until Georgia scared the crap out of her because she appeared out of nowhere. "He's back, right?"

"Yes. And stop sneaking up on me."

"I had to come up the other hall so WHR didn't see me."

Emma shook her head. "So, now we're using code."

"Well, we have to be professional up here. Clients are waiting to see their brokers." She waved her hands for Emma to move. "Get up and go fill him in on our week from hell."

Emma stopped at the breakroom to fix Colin and herself a cup of coffee. As usual, his door was open. "Coffee." She closed and locked the door behind her. She didn't put it passed Margaret to sneak in and try to listen.

His smile warmed her from head to toe. She smiled back as she approached and placed his mug on his desk, and then sat.

"Thanks for the welcome back note." He held a paper snowflake in his hand.

"You're welcome."

"The hearts were a nice touch." He winked.

"Thank you for the bonus. The ice skater was cute." She held up her mug toward him and then took a sip.

Neither of them spoke.

He studied her. "I missed this."

"I did, too." Their few moments of quiet were short-lived.

He put the mug down and laced his fingers behind his neck. "Okay, fill me in."

After one more sip, Emma started from the beginning, leaving no details out. "She wasted no time. The first thing I did was look for their employee records. They were gone."

"Have you looked since?"

"No. I've been too busy." She slumped in her chair.

"Emma, why didn't you call me?"

"How could I? Your mom was here." She pursed her lips. "You know Margaret's trying to stir things up."

He typed in his password and went to the employee records, where he found Keith and Sally's files. "They're here now."

"She put them back and there's no proof she ever removed them. I'm not supposed to be able to see they were missing."

He leaned in close to the computer monitor. "Says here, she fired them on grounds of fraternization because they didn't disclose their relationship."

"Can she do that?"

"Unfortunately, she can. They broke company policy, and she crossed all the t's and dotted the i's in her report." He rubbed his chin. Margaret's little ripple just turned into a bigger wave in his calm sea.

Emma wrung her hands. "Can she come after us?

He continued to study the monitor and then started typing. "Nope. Remember we filed our contract with H.R. and I made sure we had the blessing of Rob." He popped the arms of the chair. "I need to talk to Margaret."

"Welcome back. Finish your coffee."

"I need something stronger, but that's against company policy." He shook his head. "Just get her in here."

About forty minutes later Emma announced Ms. Rice was there to see him.

In her usual stance, she walked in and sat down. "Welcome back. I hope you had a nice week off."

"Thank you. We need to talk about what happened last week."

"I don't understand."

She planned on playing dumb again. Then in her passive-aggressive manner, she'd take her time finding someone to fill the receptionist's position, keeping his job and the office in turmoil to pay him back.

"I understand you let Mr. Freedman and Ms. Adams go." He looked her right in the eye. "Why?"

"Everything is in their files. I caught them in an embrace in the breakroom."

"Were you spying on them?"

Her hand covered her mouth. "I'd never do that."

Of course, you'd never sneak around to get what you want. How does this woman live with herself? "Then explain."

"I was getting some coffee and walked in. When I confronted them on the matter, they didn't deny anything. Mr. Freedman had a warning on his record and Ms. Adams had a warning and a write-up on hers."

For now, he'd let her explanation slide. He had more pressing matters. "Tell me what you've done about replacing Ms. Adams."

"I've posted the position and I'll be taking applications starting in two weeks."

What he knew about the hiring process, finding a full-time employee might take a month or more, including the training. She's being passive-aggressive by stretching out the process. "So, how will you handle the vacancy until then?"

"Georgia and Emma will fill the gap."

He sat back and tapped his fingernail on the desk. He wasn't willing to put Emma and Georgia through that. "No, they won't. By Wednesday I want a temp in here who can handle the job. Whoever that person is stays until the position is filled. If the temp is working out, they get a shot at the position if they want it."

"I'm not sure that's possible."

He leaned in to stare into her vacant eyes. "I think for your sake, you make it possible. That's an order and are we clear on this?"

Her eyes widened and for the first time, he denoted an emotion. She readjusted in her seat and returned to the ice lady position. "I'll find someone by Wednesday. Is there anything else?"

"No. Thank you for coming in."

She stood and walked toward the door. He waited until she was in the center of the room. "Ms. Rice."

She stopped and turned.

"Make sure the temp is capable of handling the position. I expect nothing less from you."

She nodded and left.

For the next few weeks, Colin had to make do with Emma helping with other duties to keep the office running. He didn't like seeing an empty desk from his door.

After Margaret's plan to destroy the tranquility of the office environment, Colin noticed a shift in his employee's attitudes. From his first day on the job, he'd seen groups gather in the breakroom and hear laughter throughout the day. All that came to a halt. People came in but didn't gather. They'd stayed in their spaces until lunch, and at five they'd leave.

He had a huge morale problem on his hands thanks to Ms. Rice.

Her tsunami wave was getting stronger.

By the end of October, he had Emma back full-time. He didn't like the idea that their Saturdays ended with his mother's visits but dared not ask her to dinner after Margaret's stunt. He kept his distance because he couldn't give Margaret any ammunition to use against them.

The office morale remained low during the adjustment period of training a new receptionist and reassigning Keith's clients to other brokers.

By late-October, the office morale had still not recovered from Margaret's employee firing stunt. She continued as if nothing had happened and that pissed him off. Margaret was his rotten apple in the management team that needed to be plucked before the total corporate harvest failed.

Emma brought in their coffee. Colin stopped working. She loved their few minutes of quiet every morning, Monday through Friday, and always with his office door open. Just as a precaution.

"Emma. Can you get together a Director's retreat up at the Pendleton Lodge together?"

"Yeah. If no one has it reserved."

"See what you can do. Something around here has to change."

Emma peeked up under her lashes and fixed her gaze on him.

He chuckled. "Yeah. I know. Get rid of Margaret."

"Very well said, but not so easy. No one feels comfortable around her."

"Tell me about it. At the party I had a few weeks ago, everyone was having fun. When she walked in, folks stayed around for a respectable time, then left before ten." He shook his head. "Talk about an ice queen."

"Did Sam find anything on the flash drive?"

"Not a thing. Just some pictures and her files. I gave the thing back to her."

"So, we're stuck with her until she does something noteworthy of firing."

They finished their coffee in silence.

As soon as Emma returned to her desk, she started working on the retreat plans. She drummed her fingers as she stared at the lodge's availability calendar. "This isn't good."

The only vacancy started from December 15, through the end of the year. She glanced up from her desk to see Colin working at his.

"Hey. You got time to talk?" She loved their informal communication system. "I've got some dates for you on the reservation. It's not good."

"What's wrong?

She got up and walked into his office. "December 15 is the first date you can officially use the place as a group.

"Why so late?"

"Maintenance, family visiting, and something about Charlie the caretaker needing some time off."

Colin's brows knitted. He didn't appear happy. "Get it scheduled until the twentieth."

"Do you think that's a good idea? It might make things worse. That's so close to the holidays."

"Hear me out. If Margaret doesn't play nice during those five days, she's gone. I'll be a hero around here if that happens and give everyone an early Christmas present. Here she stays locked down in her office. Up there she'll have to be front and center. I bet she doesn't hold it together and gives me what I need." Colin laid out his plan to get the directors to work as a group by cooking their meals and participating in team-building activities. Emma prayed Margaret wouldn't be able to pass muster.

"Is Charlie easy to work with?

"You'll love him. He's like a giant teddy bear."

"Okay. I'll call him to see what I can work out, then get this scheduled."

Colin was right. Charlie was a dream come true as caretakers go. He ran down everything he'd need to have the lodge ready for their arrival.

Emma reached over to turn on her desk lamp and then got up to turn off the overhead lights. She walked over to the lamps on either side of the couch in front of the windows.

The days had gotten shorter with the approach of winter and in the dimly lit room, she watched the first early snowfall of the season beyond the windows. Fluffy specks fell on their graceful descent to the ground. For Emma, their appearance meant she'd soon take to the ice on the pond behind her apartment.

She took a moment before she returned to her desk. She'd worked all day on the details for the retreat. The time came to fill in her boss and then end her day.

"It's snowing."

Colin's face went white and he stopped working on the computer to securitize the windows.

"What's wrong?"

"Oh. I'm just a little concerned."

"Why?"

"Will it cover the streets?"

"Not for a while. It's too early for it to stick." His statements and behavior puzzled her.

He stared at the windows and then waved a hand. "Come on let's get this done."

She laid the upstairs floor plan in front of him. "Charlie sent me a layout of the interior. I assigned the bedrooms and gave you the biggest one."

From the papers in her hand, she laid down the food list. "I tried to select foods that were easy to prepare yet had a gourmet flare. Here's the wine and beverage list and the travel arrangements for the group. You'll fly into Calgary. Charles will meet them with the van and drive them to the lodge."

He took a few minutes to review her work. "Emma, this is impressive, but you forgot something."

"What?" Her gaze darted over the papers and she rearranged them.

He tapped his finger over the last upstairs bedroom. "This one's for you. You're coming with."

"Why?"

"I'm your boss. Do I need a reason?"

She tapped him on the shoulder. "Yes."

"Hey." He rubbed her finger's point of contact.

"That didn't hurt." She stared at him. "Tell me why?"

His hand messaged the area her hand made contact. "Because I want you there and besides, you need a break."

She sucked in some air. "It'd be more fun without you-know-who."

He sported a huge grin. "I know. We'll just have to make do and pray for the best."

He arranged the papers in a stack. "Now, for the hard part. Set up a Director's meeting for tomorrow afternoon. So I can break the news."

He turned off his computer, packed his briefcase, and headed for the closet.

"Come on. I have to leave. Out."

"What's the rush?" In a few seconds, she stood next to him as he locked the door.

"I've never driven in snow." He gave her a teeth-flashing smile and left.

Colin dropped the news on his four directors. At first none of them said anything. He attempted to act enthusiastic about the event, but the three directors with families weren't falling for his ruse. As he expected, Margaret was the only one the timeframe didn't faze.

Several encouraged him to wait until spring and cited some good reasons. He wished he could tell them what he hoped for, but that would kill his plan.

"Think of this as a mini-vacation at the expense of the company." All he got was grumbles. Margaret said nothing.

Colin walked out of the meeting and had his fill of office politics. He needed a break.

At his desk, he did an internet searched for activities near and around Calgary that involved the Canadian Rockies. He moved on to ski resorts. "Skiing. Perfect."

He'd given some thought to asking Emma to join him then dropped the idea. He imagined her snow bunny look and knew he'd have trouble keeping his hands to himself. Next year, she'd be free to join him if she wanted and if his plans for Margaret worked.

After he finalized his trip's arrangements, he called Emma into his office. "I'm taking off a few days early to try my hand at skiing."

"Oh." Her face lost the glow he'd come accustomed to seeing. "When do you leave?"

"Six days before the retreat. I need time to pack and then I'll drive."

She showed no emotion. Over the past months he grew to recognize her facial expressions. This one wasn't good. "Emma, are you okay?"

She took a deep breath. "I'm afraid of what Margaret might try."

He understood her concern and took a chance, a big chance. "You want to come with me."

She froze. Only her mouth opened.

Yep. He blew it.

"Colin. What are you asking?"

"I'm just saying, if you're not here, you don't have to deal with any office politics."

Her lips made a half-crescent. "Then we leave Georgia by herself. I can't do that to her but thank you for the invitation. You go. If she gives me any problems, I'll figure it out."

"Look. I'll make it clear to her that no changes of any kind take place without my permission. She has to wait until I get back."

"And if she doesn't listen?"

"She's gone for disobeying a direct order. I'll make sure she understands."

The color returned to her complexion. "Have fun."

CHAPTER 13

THE VIBRATIONS BEGAN with the steering wheel as Colin hugged the curve of the mountain road in his Mercedes. He leaned forward, trying to listen. *Was the problem with the road or the car?* The low rumble grew louder and the car began to shake. To his left, the noise intensified into a roar as a wall of snow barreled downhill, right for him. His reflexes kicked in, and he punched the accelerator. With one eye on the road and the other on the avalanche, Colin judged his speed on the slick pavement. He had to make it to the other side of this monster, or he'd be dead.

Heart rate in overdrive, he gripped the steering wheel so hard his knuckles blanched. Beads of sweat formed on his brow, but he dared not lift a hand to swipe at the droplets.

Balls of snow, of varying sizes, bounced off the pavement in front, to the side, and behind the car. In a few more seconds, he'd be covered. Forget the avalanche. He needed to concentrate on the road and slammed the gas pedal to the floor. Sadie exceeded his expectations. In the rearview mirror, he watched the cascading snow cover and block the road.

A sigh passed his lips, confident he'd beaten the terror until a thud came from the rear passenger side.

The sudden force pushed the back of the car into the empty oncoming lane.

Hard snow pelted the canvas roof and covered the windshield. He swerved and corrected. Another glance in the rearview mirror confirmed his suspicion. The rear of his beloved car collided with a snowball the size of Texas.

Adrenaline coursed through his veins as he drove up the mountain pass, determined not to stop until he reached his destination, the Pendleton Lodge.

Twenty minutes later, Colin pulled into the driveway.

When he left Toronto, he'd planned a nice scenic drive across Canada. Death by avalanche was not part of his strategy. He shook out his trembling hands and then rubbed them together. After multiple long breaths, his pulse slowed and his hands changed from pale white to pink. He lowered his lids, sucked in more cold air, exhaled, and exited the car. His knees wobbled for a second. He took in more breaths until he stood firm. Fine swirls of frozen mist formed in front of his face and took the time to span the landscape.

In the dead of winter, the grounds appeared mystical, covered in a mantle of white snow. A dense quiet engulfed the terrain which was different from his last visit to the lodge during the summer months a few years ago.

The snow crunched under his feet as he made his way to the passenger side to examine the damage from the giant snowball. "Damn it! Sadie, I'm sorry."

He slammed his hand on the trunk, then ran his fingers over the depression. He stood, stepped back, and inspected for more dents, but found nothing. A puff of mist escaped from his mouth. He shook his head. "That's going to cost me a few bucks that I didn't need to spend right now."

One press of the fob opened the trunk as his cell rang.

"Hey, Junior." Colin couldn't ignore the opportunity to tug at his best friend's chain. Robert did the same whenever he had the opportunity. Neither resisted the chance to be boys even though both were thirty-one. Colin lifted his bag out and lowered it to the ground. Snow compacted under the weight.

"Stop calling me that."

"How else can I tell you apart from your dad?"

"That's why we call him Rob."

Colin chuckled. He just loved pulling that chain.

"Did you make it to Banff?"

Colin swiped the back of his neck and closed the trunk before letting out a... "No. A last-minute change of plans."

"Where are you?"

"The lodge." Colin leaned against the back wheel well. He'd lead Robert on just enough to mess with him before he'd tell him the complete story.

"I thought you were going to ski Mt. Norquay and stay in Banff?"

"Yeah, that was the plan." Colin played with his misty breath, trying to form rings, with no success.

"What happened?"

From his worried tone, He decided to fill Robert in. "I decided to stay here and drive back and forth to the resort down the road. I figured why pay for a room when I had your dad's place at my disposal?"

"So you made it."

Colin gave the proverbial chain another tug by not divulging too much information. "Barely."

"What do you mean, barely? Did you have car trouble or something?"

"More like the something."

Robert didn't speak, nor did Colin. Just one more tug.

"Okay. What's the something?"

The cold nipped at Colin's nose and this conversation needed to end soon. The warmth of a roaring fire called to him. "The snowfall from last night caused an avalanche. I'm locked in until the road clears and my skiing on fresh powder is toast."

"Avalanche?"

"The darn thing almost got me."

"You're okay?"

"Still shaken up." Colin looked down at his trembling hand. "But not hurt. The car's a bit banged up." Colin walked to the side of the car to re-inspect the depression and shook his head.

"Dude, is there anything I can do?"

"No, I should be fine. I might have to cancel the retreat."

"That's not good."

"No kidding." *Not good?* He'd planned the retreat to advance his career and repair the damage his H.R. Director had inflicted. He covered one of his freezing ears with his hand and kicked at the snow. "I'd hoped to impress your dad and lock down the future president position."

Robert snorted. "That's yours. Dad already decided. Besides, do you think Mom would forgive him if he didn't give it to you? After all, Bro, you're their adopted son."

"I know, but I already screwed up by scheduling the retreat to begin on December 15th. No one wants to go on a fun corporate event right before the holidays." To get Margaret to act out was his trump card to give him grounds to dismiss her. If his plan worked, his employees would love him. "If clearing the road takes too long, I'll have no choice but to cancel."

Colin surveyed the immediate area, starting over his left shoulder and moving to the right. The almost diminished thumping in his chest started to increase. "Do you know if an avalanche can hit this place? I don't want to wake up buried in snow."

"No chance. Dad knew what he was doing when he picked the site. The area is flat and safe."

Colin made another scan of the snowy landscape to convince himself before he let his shoulders relax. "Good."

"Did Charlie stock the place?"

"I'm still outside. According to Emma, he said the place would be ready by today. So, if it's not, I may ask you to send me a lifeline."

"If Charlie said today, it's ready."

"How are things between you and Emma? Too bad she couldn't get off to join you on the ski trip."

Colin almost dropped his phone. "What are you saying? I have a business relationship with her and nothing else."

A hardy laugh errupted. "Whatever you say, but you're lucky to have her."

Robert had no idea how lucky. Emma was a man's dream of a near-perfect woman even though their relationship never veered off the path.

A gust of wind blew bitter cold air around Colin and the tips of his ears and fingers stung. "I better get going."

"Call if you need anything. I'll keep that lifeline handy."

"Knowing you, all you'll do is send me a Saint Bernard." With his bag in tow, he trudged toward the back door.

"They carry bourbon."

"Good point, but so does your dad's stocked bar in the game room of this grand palace."

Robert huffed. "I'll give that to Dad, he does know his bourbon."

"Tell him thank you for me." He reached the back door and punched in the key code. "I'm at the door. If I run into any trouble I'll call. Later."

The floor-to-ceiling windows in the back of the great room allowed light to fill the massive two-story space. Pine boards covered the walls and ceiling. A massive antler chandelier hung from the center cross beam, the symbol of any respectable mountain lodge.

Colin walked toward the glass wall. In the distance lay a frozen lake with a mountain vista beyond. He combed the area for any signs of snow accumulation on the closest mountain slopes.

Rob had chosen wisely when picking the site. The flat topography sheltered the building from any threat of an avalanche's crushing blow.

His stomach rumbled and turned his attention to the kitchen. "Time to see if Charlie and Emma were on their game." Without food, he might be in real trouble. He headed to the fridge and opened the door. His mouth curled up. His executive assistant and the caretaker had done their jobs. They'd stocked the refrigerator and pantry to the max.

"Hmm. Charlie even heated the place." He glanced back to the fireplace and smiled. A stack of firewood lay ready for a warm fire and a glass of that bourbon.

All he needed to do was get comfortable and wait.

Despite the weight of his bag, he took the steps two at a time toward the bedroom Emma assigned to him.

Since he moved to Canada, he'd grown close to Emma. This corporate retreat was his plan to get closer to his management staff. If the blocked road shattered his objective, fine dining by himself served no purpose and he found himself in an unplanned prison. He guessed the alcohol might help.

Emma finished lacing her right skate and checked the left. With everything ready for the management retreat, she allowed herself time to indulge in her passion—skating. At the edge of the lake, the view from the bench spanned the snow-covered mountains. She'd preferred the rugged terrain drenched in the scent of pine over the smells of the steel jungle in which she lived. An inhalation of crisp clean air expanded her chest. She held her breath to savor the moment the released the air from deep in her lungs.

The white peaks in the distance jetted against the clear blue sky. Soft clouds floated like a flock of fluffy white sheep across the horizon. As far as she was concerned, she was in heaven.

At the ice's edge, she pushed off, the blades coasted across the surface, unimpeded. The brisk air bit her cheeks. In her element, free from stress, she allowed her mind to clear.

The drumbeat in her ears pounded as she performed a figure eight, and then spun into an upright spin. The twirling motion caused her short plaid skirt to flare out from her thighs. She tucked her arms which increased the velocity of the spin.

She ground the skate's toe pick into the ice to stop. With her arms crossed over her, she closed her eyes and tilted her head back to allow the sun to settle across her face.

The cold penetrated her beige leggings and sent a shiver up her spine. As her respirations slowed, she opened her eyes and inhaled the bouquet of mountain air. She'd never experienced skating outside of the city, and this little piece of heaven allowed her to forget her stressors.

The next few days, she'd pamper herself with soaks in the hot tub, read a romance novel, and have all the skate time she wanted before the directors arrived.

Margaret wasn't happy when Emma told her Charlie needed help and that Emma had to leave four days early for the lodge. Emma had lied, a tiny white lie

because she needed time to herself. Colin's planned ski trip left her at Margaret's mercy despite his efforts to protect her. The lie saved her from the Witch's insults. So, with Georgia's blessing, she fibbed and left.

Emma scanned the view. Who wouldn't be relaxed in a setting like this? She pushed to make a few circles around the outer rim of the ice. With each kick, she increased her speed and the circles tightened until she ended in another spin, this time a camel.

An hour later, Emma made her way to the bench and removed her skates. She took a moment to watch the setting sun cast purple and blue hues over the mountain range. She didn't care if the cold nipped, she'd never tire of the freshness. Then her stomach growled and she patted her abdomen. "Okay, let's go eat."

She entered the lodge on the lower level and walked into the game room. As she passed the pool table, she picked up the cue ball and propelled it toward the triangular cluster at the other end.

The white ball struck the grouping and scattered them in a random configuration over the table. The clack from the force reminded her of a bar filled with patrons she occasionally visited with Georgia after work. On their girls' night out, the bar was a place were she blew off steam and could be herself away from her structured corporate life.

She stopped at the stocked bar along the right side of the room just past the wall of windows and poured herself two fingers of bourbon into a crystal highball glass. With a pass of the glass under her nose, she savored the sweet aroma that floated up and teased her senses.

Yep, getting tipsy was on tonight's agenda. She had four days before Colin and the management team arrived and planned on enjoying every second. After dinner, she'd come back downstairs, start up the hot tub, pour herself another glass of bourbon, and soak away any remaining stress or sore muscles from the extended bout of skating.

On the main floor, she walked to her bedroom down a short hallway near the kitchen. She'd decided to switch rooms from the sixth bedroom upstairs that Colin had assigned to her. This downstairs one put some distance between her, the

directors, and Colin.

Since she wasn't management, she'd have no part in the team-building exercises, and the second the team entered, she'd fade into the background as the executive assistant of the company's future president. She likened the experience to the old saying *'Children are better seen than heard'* but on a business level. The invisibility didn't bother her unless the head of H.R. was involved. That woman had a way of triggering buttons that opened old wounds.

She stripped and clad herself in a flannel mid-calf robe, then downed the rest of the bourbon. She studied the glass. "That Rob Pendleton sure knows his liquor." A slight upper movement represented a toast. "To Rob. Thank you, I needed this."

Her cell chirped and Emma snatched it off the bed. Glad to hear from her bestie, she placed Georgia on speaker. "Hey, girl. How are things?"

"Getting some skating in? Knowing you, that's all you've done."

She plopped on her back across the black and white buffalo plaid comforter spread on the bed. "You know me too well."

"Yep, ever since we were kids, you took to those skates like a duck to water. Except, more like frozen water. So what time do you expect The Suits?"

"Their plane lands around noon, so maybe sometime later afternoon on the 15th

"Enjoy yourself until then. You've been working so much I haven't had time to see you."

"I know, and I'm sorry about that. I promise I'll do better after the first of the year." She fiddled with a moose tail made of yarn on a red and black plaid pillow. "Planning this thing took so much time and stoking all the Director's egos was like herding cats. None of them wanted to come and they all let me know at every chance. You wouldn't believe the excuses they came up with."

Georgia giggled. "And I'm sure you made it very clear they had no choice. Hey. Speaking of the first of the year, when's the grand opening?"

Emma clenched her teeth and then let out a sigh. "Not for a bit yet. Maybe this spring or summer if the online store keeps growing."

"Emma, not again. You've already pushed your plans back. How many

times, six or seven? Come on. You know with my social media connections, I can help more."

"You are helping. That's why the orders keep coming in. I know *#cheekyreviews* is your baby, but the money isn't quite there for my baby. The opening of Emma's Attic will have to wait a few more months."

Every time she worked the numbers, they came up short even after Colin's generous checks for helping him. She had to wait. Her financial plan consisted of one year's operating costs and living expenses to make sure her dream of a shabby-chic antique store near the upscale neighborhood of Leaside in Toronto succeeded. Without enough money the shop remained on hold. Emma continued to be stuck in a job where the only saving grace was her wonderful boss, Colin, and her beastie, Georgia.

"Hey, don't knock my Social Media presence. My viewers love me." She paused. "You know, I really think you don't want to be your own boss."

Georgia's words caught her off guard. "Of course, I do. I just don't want to fail."

"Yeah, I get it, but you've gotta let go of what happened with your ex."

Her ex. No matter how hard she tried, his cruel words crawled in and disrupted her confidence when she least expected it. "Let's change the subject. I want nothing to ruin the few days I have to myself."

"Sorry. When's Dreamboat arriving?"

"You changed his name again?" Emma flipped onto her stomach.

"Duh. I'll never get over that 6'4", sandy-colored hair, a bod to die for, glacier blue-eyed hunk. His eyes alone should be all it takes to suck you in, knowing how much you like frozen water."

"Georgia, you're not funny. Whether I'm attracted to him or not, nothing will ever happen. You know I need this job, and the money it provides while I get my permits in order and buy the shop's inventory."

"Maybe you'll never open your shop because you can't leave Dreamboat."

Her mind reeled at the words. Could Georgia be on to something? She did love seeing Colin every morning, and his glacier blues did suck her in. *No. No way.* "No, I don't think so."

"Right. Well, when does he get there?"

"When the rest of the team does. Remember he's in Banff skiing."

Emma froze. A noise came from the kitchen. Ear cocked toward the door, and she waited. Another sound. She gasped and flung her hand over her mouth. Her skin prickled. Her hands trembled. Her pulse thundered.

"Georgia, I think someone is in the house. I'm keeping the phone on but putting it in my pocket. If something happens, call the police."

"You can't go out there. Just call the police and wait for them."

"Hang on." A quick scan of the room yielded the closest weapon, a candlestick lamp with a heavy square base. With care not to make noise, she yanked at the plug, tore off the shade, and removed the light bulb. She grabbed the neck to use the base as a weapon.

After a few practice swings, she was confident she'd do some damage. "I'm going to go check."

"Emma, don't!"

"Shhh. Call the police if this goes bad. I'll keep you on speaker so you can hear." She slipped the phone into her pocket.

"Emma, I don't like this."

"Be quiet or I'll hang up and my death will be on your hands."

The wood door warmed her cheek as she pressed her ear to the surface. Pots clanged and someone rifled through drawers. A slow rotation of the knob opened the door to a crack. She peered down the hall and saw a light on in the kitchen.

Her mouth felt like cotton and she had trouble swallowing. She inched her way down the hallway. In a few more feet, she'd be near the kitchen.

"Emma! Emma!" Georgia started screaming over the phone. Dang her! She could never follow instructions. If she could hear her, so could the intruder.

She fumbled in her pocket and pulled out the phone then whispered, "If I die, I'll haunt you." She hung up.

The noises from the kitchen stopped. *Oh no. They know I'm here.* She hugged the wall and raised the lamp, ready to strike.

CHAPTER 14

"OH, CRAP!" COLIN gripped his upper arm, spun from the pain, and stumbled. He managed to remain upright with the help of the kitchen counter. The adrenaline effect went into hyper drive and instinct took over.

He grabbed a cast-iron frying pan off the counter and spun to face his assailant. With both hands on the handle, he raised the pan over his shoulder. He blinked twice. "Emma? What the hell are you doing here, and why did you hit me?"

Emma froze, her mouth agape. She let the lamp fall to the floor and rushed to him. "I thought you were trying to rob the place."

She grabbed his good arm to guide him to the dining area. "Sit and let me see."

"Geez. This hurts." He massaged his upper arm as he plopped in one of the chairs around the dining area table.

"Take off your shirt."

"Yes, dear." Inside he kicked himself for making that inappropriate comment. In the office, he thought of her as his work-wife. Heck, they bickered like a married couple.

He'd make comments. She'd snap back a quick retort. But deep down, their private banter lifted his spirits, and was always playful and respectful, but this was not the time or place to step over that line.

"Colin. Not now."

He complied, pulling the long-sleeved, fleece tee over his head to reveal a bluing deltoid muscle.

"Oh, no. Don't move." Emma raced around the kitchen in search of something to use as an ice bag. She opened drawers until she found a zip-lock bag, filled it with ice, and wrapped it in a kitchen towel. She placed the bag next to Colin's shoulder.

"Easy." He grimaced as the cold touched his skin.

"I'm so sorry. I hope nothing's broken." She held the ice bag to the forming bruise.

"You mean like that lamp? If I wasn't taller than you, I'd be on the floor with my head bashed in." He reached up to adjust the pack and covered Emma's hand. His gaze settled on her bust line. A sliver of the swell of her breast peeked out. For months he fantasized about how she'd look dressed like she was. He wanted to run his fingers over her soft skin, to caress every inch of her body.

His injured hand moved so he could dig his fingers into the couch cushion. Nope, he had to stop, or he'd be spending way too much time taking cold showers. Ever since he'd found her sleeping on the couch in his office, he'd been hooked. For the past nine months, he'd watched her graceful movements as she went about her daily office routine.

Even though it frustrated him, he'd never acted on the impulse because of the company's fraternization policy. If he kept himself in check, he'd at least maintain a working relationship with her. What else would an honorable man do?

She released her grip on the pack and pulled her robe tighter around her body. "What are you doing here?"

"I changed my mind about staying in Banff and decided I'd stay here and drive every morning to the resort down the road." He wouldn't tell her he was unwilling to spend the money on the room rental when he had free accommodations. She didn't need to know his thrifty side trumped better skiing.

"And I could ask the same."

"I told Margaret I had to come up to help Charlie and took an earlier flight. With you gone, I had nothing to do at the office. I saw an opportunity for some free time alone. Obviously, I was wrong."

He snickered. "If I knew I was going to be taking my life into my hands, I might have come up with the others. Kinda like safety in numbers." He adjusted the pack.

She hugged her waist and expelled air from her lungs in a huff. "Stop it. How can I make this up to you?"

With all his heart, he wanted to tell her sleeping with him would heal all his wounds, but he wasn't that kind of guy. "What about Georgia."

"She ordered me to leave."

"Before you left was Margaret behaving herself?"

"Unfortunately, yes."

"Damn."

"I know."

"Have you eaten?"

"No, I just got in from skating and planned on fixing something once I changed."

Her chestnut hair framed her flawless face. She'd never worn her hair down at the office or on their sale excursions. He liked the look. She was stunning.

He studied the robe. She had to change into something more substantial or he'd risk losing his self-control. "Looks like I interrupted you. Why don't you go get dressed and we can make something together?"

She hesitated and caught her lower lip between her teeth. "I've got an idea. Come with me." She reached for his good arm and tugged for him to stand. "You lie on the couch and keep that arm iced."

Once he was prone, she found two throw pillows. She knelt next to the couch. "Raise your head." Inches from his face, her warm breath caressed his lips. As she adjusted the pillows, for a second she stopped and focused on his eyes. Her lips parted. Then with one breath, she stood and broke the bond. She grabbed a throw and covered him. "I won't be long."

His pulse sped up. Did she just react to him? When she stooped to pick up the lamp, the back of her robe rose to barely cover her bottom.

He nearly choked when he swallowed. Body parts below his belt jumped alive. The sway of her hips stayed in his line of sight until she faded into the darkness of the hallway. "Hey, where are you going? You're bedrooms upstairs."

"I changed that. Tell you later."

Thank heaven she didn't walk up the stairs. He might have gotten an eye full under that short robe. How could he spend the next several days alone with her? He swiped his hand over his face because he knew he was a doomed man.

Emma closed the door behind her and leaned against the smooth surface. Her inner voice screamed in her head, "You can't be alone with him!"

For nine months, she'd wished she could tell him how she felt, but she needed her job. Staying on a professional level with Colin was an act of pure discipline. The sparks she'd experienced around him were kept under wraps by the physical presence of the others. But now? What would stop her?

Why did she get so close to him? Just the thought of him caused her girly parts to twitch.

She had to get a grip and stay focused on her goal. Her plan was within reach and she needed her income to open her shop in late spring or early summer. Her current business plan had no place for an early termination because she and her boss became too friendly. Why? Why? Why did she have to work for him?

She stopped at the wall mirror that hung next to the bathroom. Her mouth dropped open. She resembled an advertisement for a phone sex date in a robe that hung loosely around her chest and a hem that fell low enough to preserve her modesty. In a dash, she combed the closet for the least sexy thing she'd brought, a baggy sweater and a ratty pair of yoga pants.

Her phone vibrated. "Georgia. I'm sorry I hung up."

"Are you okay? Who was it?"

Emma knew a full explanation was in order, but she didn't have time. "Colin."

Static came over the phone. "Eye Candy is there? Alone with you?"

"Georgia, stop. I can't talk right now. I'll call before I go to bed.

"Promise? No matter how late?"

"Promise. I have to go." Emma hung up and tucked the phone into her pocket.

She walked past the full-length mirror, stopped, and took a few steps back to check the new wardrobe choice. Her hair cascaded around her shoulders. That wouldn't due. After her robe mishap, she needed to tone down her looks but in comfortable attire. With a few twists of a scrunchie, she sported a serious bun on top of her head. She patted the wadded mess and bounced twice on the balls of her feet as she turned and headed for the great room.

Colin appeared asleep and she decided not to disturb him. That was the least she could do after clobbering him. In the kitchen, she pulled together a salad, sautéed two perch filets, and steamed fresh green beans. A bottle of wine and crusty bread completed the meal.

She stood over him and analyzed his face. The lines had softened. He appeared younger. Strands of disheveled sandy hair fell over his forehead. She reached to brush one of the misplaced strands but stopped and withdrew her hand. "Colin, dinner is ready."

He half-smile and squinted before running a hand over his face. "You made dinner?" His nose searched. "Whatever it is, it smells good."

"You needed the rest. It's nothing fancy. Do you need help getting up?"

"No." He ran his fingers through his hair, pushing the stray hairs back into place. Then he grabbed the ice pack and swung his legs over the edge of the couch. The throw slipped to expose his bare, chiseled chest.

Emma almost died. Earlier, she had concentrated on easing the man's pain and missed the six-pack abs. She'd always admired his build under his tailored suits or close-fitted tees on their furniture-hunting excursions. Now, she witnessed the bare essence of what filled out those clothes. Her mouth gaped as she sucked in the air. Her desire for her boss went into overdrive.

No. No. No. After her ex-husband's betrayal, the charms of any man needed to be kept at bay. But other than her ex, she'd never seen any half-naked men. Colin was the first and eye candy didn't describe him at all.

Nope. Sexy boss or not, she'd never make the same mistake again. Emma's Attic would open and she'd be in control of her life.

Colin dropped the ice pack to fling the throw over his shoulder. "I think I need a shirt that buttons."

"Right. Did you bring one?"

"Yep." He nudged his head toward the second story. "The closet in my bedroom."

She dashed up the stairs and found a front-buttoned flannel. She held the hanger up to study the shirt. "You'll do, warm, practical, and a good lust deterrent."

With one yank she pulled the shirt free from the hanger and raced back to find Colin still sitting on the couch, clutching the ice pack to his shoulder.

"Put this arm in." She slid the first sleeve over the injured arm, then over the good arm.

Now came the hard part, trying not to react when she buttoned the shirt.

She pulled the shirt edges to close the gap and worked her way up, one button at a time. His firm ab muscles flexed with each tug and button meeting buttonhole.

A slight sigh escaped as she reached the last button. Face to face, she kept her sight on her fumbling fingers. His balmy breath brushed across her cheek. They'd never been this close except for that time he clipped her cheek with his arm. Then, exposed skin wasn't involved.

Every ounce of willpower went into pushing the last button through the buttonhole, but she completed the task and stood. Able to compose herself, she said, "Let's eat and you can finish icing after dinner."

At the dining table, he pulled out a chair for Emma. "Thank you for cooking and for letting me sleep. By the way, I didn't see your rental car."

"Charlie gave me the code to the garage. There's a free bay. Tomorrow, you should pull Sadie in."

"We're your skis?"

"I don't have any. I planned on renting this time. If I liked taking my life in my hands as I soared down a slope on toothpicks, I'd considered buying some in the future." He settled across from her and poured two glasses of wine. He raised his. "To us and our ability to survive our unconventional greeting."

She chuckled and clinked her glass against his.

"Two adrenaline rushes are too much for my system."

Emma cocked her head. "Two rushes?"

His brows knitted. "With all the pleasantries we exchanged—"

"Would you stop? I said I was sorry, let you sleep, and cooked you dinner."

"You're right." He raised his glass and took a swig.

"You're forgiven." She picked up her knife and fork to cut her fish. "So, other than the two of us trying to kill each other, what was the other rush?"

"I almost got buried by an avalanche."

CHAPTER 15

THE CLANG OF Emma's knife hitting the plate echoed through the massive room. She stopped. Her throat tightened. "Avalanche?"

He placed his palms on the table. "Yep, a few kilometers down the road." He filled her in on the details down to the damage to Sadie.

She sat back in her chair. Tightness in her lungs made her ache. His cavalier attitude confused her. What if he'd died? She might not have found out for days. The squeeze under her ribs clenched tighter. Could she live without seeing him every day?

"Emma, are you okay?" He reached across the table for her hand.

"Yeah." Her fingers laced through his. "I'm glad you're all right."

A silly half grin appeared. "I'm tellin' you it was a mind-blower and something I never want to experience again."

"Colin." Her voice wavered and tears welled. "Don't do this."

"What?"

"You could've died."

"I know, but I didn't."

Unbelievable, that he remained so calm. She released his hand and pushed away from the table. She was mad at him for his cavalier attitude. Fluid moistened her lids. From the counter, she retrieved her phone. A quick swipe of her eyes took care of the waiting tears. She filled her lungs and exhaled. After a few taps on the screen, she found information about the progress of the snow removal.

She switched into work mode. “Have you contacted the rest of the team to fill them in?”

“Not yet.”

She glanced up from the phone. “Did you check your cell for a signal?”

“I talked to Robert earlier, but then I got sideswiped.” He knitted his brow and added a puppy dog stare as he ran his hand over his injured shoulder.

She planted her free hand on her hip and glared. “Now you’re milking it.”

The arc of a partial smile formed. He raised his hands and gave a nod to concede.

She went back to her search. “According to this, there were two different avalanches on the road to the lodge about sixteen kilometers apart. The one closest to town should take a day to clear.” She read on. Butterflies fluttered in her stomach. She covered her mouth and walked toward the table.

“Oh. N0. We need to call the police to let them know we’re here. There were several avalanches on different roads. According to this, your avalanche might take the longest to clear since the road isn’t traveled much during the winter.”

Colin’s face lost all expression. “That’s not good.”

“Ya think? All the planning for this event would’ve been a waste if we can’t get your team here.” She froze. “Think of the rumors when people find out we were stuck up here together.”

He pulled out his phone. “Don’t think about that now. I’ll call Margaret. She’ll have to keep the rest of the team updated. You call the police.”

Margaret, and her nose-in-the-air attitude. She hated the idea that Colin had to depend on her, and she had to subject herself to that woman in the close confines of the lodge. She was one of the reasons Emma decided to come earlier. Taking the plane from Toronto to Calgary, she could survive, but not the three-hour drive to the lodge. Never.

She placed a finger on her cheek. “I’ll call Charlie to let him know we’re okay. I wouldn’t want him to worry.”

Emma moved to the living room to make her calls.

Colin laid his phone on the table and watched Emma. He chuckled to himself at the hand gestures she used to emphasize her points while she paced. Her passion for detail made her the perfect wife. No—work-wife. He covered his mouth, surprised at his goof.

Over the past months, he'd grown to trust her, knowing she'd have his back.

The H.R. director was the exact opposite. They merely tolerated each other. After her stunt, he didn't like that her position made her second in command at the office.

Despite her show of respect, she despised him. She was like a snake waiting to attack, and everyone in the office knew that about her. So they stayed clear, which kept the office morale in turmoil.

In the next few days, and if his plan worked, the atmosphere at work would change and he'd be hailed as a miracle worker.

Emma tucked her phone into her pocket as she walked toward the dining table. "Okay, the police needed a little convincing, but they assured me they'd have the road cleared in four days. Charlie thanked me for calling."

He tapped his phone. "I wasn't as successful. Margaret didn't answer. I left her a text to call me ASAP. And if she is true to form, she'll call soon." He mimicked a few of Emma's hand gestures. Her stare told him she was close to her limit.

"Now we wait." She walked around the counter, refilled the ice pack, and handed it to Colin. "Okay, back to icing."

"How about you sit and I'll clean up the kitchen?"

The ice pack shoved at him signaled that Emma ignored his suggestion. In their relationship, he'd learned that when she was at the helm, he'd better back away.

Colin took the pack and headed for the couch. "If you need anything, I'll be right over here, relaxing with my ice pack."

The wine, down-filled sofa pillows, and decreasing adrenaline proved too much. Colin drifted off. He had no idea how long he rested in dreamland until he heard an angel call to him.

No, angels don't shake your shoulder.

He opened one eye to find Emma standing over him with his phone in her hand.

"Your phone is ringing. It's Margaret."

He grabbed the phone. Still half asleep, he ran his hand over his face and jumped to his feet.

"Hello, Margaret." He walked to the wall of windows and delved into the story of the blocked road and how the retreat might be canceled. He asked her to hold off and not tell the rest of the team because if they cleared the road before the team's arrival date, he'd proceed as planned. If the road clearance took a day longer, then he'd cancel.

A one-day delay might push the retreat too close to Christmas. He understood the importance of family and didn't want to keep the team away from theirs.

"Well, that's done."

"Are you canceling?"

"Not yet."

The prospect of spending four days with Emma and pulling off the retreat might be too much to expect. He'd wait until he had more information. Until then, he'd enjoy her company despite the hands-off work policy and Margaret's possible threats over their temporary living arrangement.

He checked out the kitchen and the crackling fire Emma had started. "You've been busy."

"You want another glass of wine?" She held a bottle.

"Thank you. I would."

In the fire's glow, he watched Emma. Her slender fingers wrapped around the bottle with ease as she bent at the waist to pour. Movements, he'd watched many times at an office desk, appeared more graceful in the flickering light of the flames. Emma was beautiful and smart. What would he do if she ever left him?

"Here you are." She handed him a glass and sat in one of the wing-backed chairs in front of the fireplace.

He took a seat in the matching chair across from her and stretched out his long legs, almost touching the river-stone hearth. He swallowed a sip of wine. "Hmm. We have four days alone ahead of us. How should we spend our time together? Any ideas, Em?" That was the first time he ever called her Em.

CHAPTER 16

LIGHT FILTERED IN and Emma peeked at the clock, 10 a.m. She couldn't remember the last time she'd slept in, and talking to Georgia half the night didn't help. But Georgia needed every minor detail before she agreed to hang up.

The memory of the night before had swirled in her head and made for a fitful sleep. She and Colin had talked to until late into the early morning as they shared a bottle of wine in front of the cozy fire.

She sensed he welcomed the relaxing time as much as she did.

With one jerk of the drapes, a view of the lake came into focus. A frosty haze hovered over the ice as the morning light reflected off the distant mountain range. The vista was spectacular for a city girl who'd never tire of the scene.

Butterflies stormed the pit of her stomach. For weeks, she'd been so busy planning the retreat that she'd abandoned her normal skate time. But for the next few days, she'd have her fill.

Out came a turtleneck, an oversized off-white cable-knit sweater, and a pair of floral print leggings. She pulled on a pair of fluffy socks. An excellent combination to provide warmth while skating and modesty in front of her very attractive boss. Oh, yeah, Colin, with whom she'd be alone for the next few days.

She picked her skating skirt and tights up from the floor where she left them the night before. "Too bad. For now you are retired and will remain in the drawer. You just might give him some bad ideas."

Next she pulled her hair into a ponytail and centered it. A crescent smile formed at the glimpse of her reflection in the mirror. With no make-up, her hair pulled back, and in baggy clothes—she exuded not one ounce of sex appeal. Her relationship with Colin had to remain low-key despite how her skin prickled, and her stomach knotted every time he came close.

A marvelous aroma tantalized her nostrils as they caught a whiff. Coffee. Her day didn't start until she drank her first kick-your-butt cup. Today would be no exception. She headed for the kitchen.

"Good morning." Colin placed a mug on the counter. "Two sugars and a touch of heavy cream."

"How do you know how I like it?" She always got their coffee in the morning. So, how?

He pushed the mug in her direction and gave a quick wink. "I never give away my secrets."

Emma sipped her coffee. "You did a good job." She spotted the chopped veggies displayed on the countertop. "What's all this?"

"Omelets. You interested?"

"Sure." She slipped onto a stool in front of the counter and watched Colin's version of a home cooking show unfold before her. He moved from the prep area to the refrigerator, the stove, and back. This man knew his way around a kitchen, and that amazed her.

From all the times they spent at his place when she helped him decorate, he never showed a domestic side. However, he was quick with his phone ordering.

First, he cracked the eggs with one hand, beat them to perfection, added a pinch of a few spices, and poured the mixture into a pan. He passed his hand over the selection of white bowls filled with red onions, green peppers, cheese, mushrooms, and bacon. "What is your desire?"

Emma pursed her lips, then pointed. "This one, this one, and that one."

Colin sprinkled the right amounts over the eggs before folding them to perfection. After a minute, he slid the show-stopping omelet onto a plate and added a split orange slice and grapes to the side. He slid the plate in front of her. "Start eating while I make mine. No sense in yours getting cold."

She took a bite. His fluffy breakfast melted in her mouth. “This is delicious. Where’d you learn to cook?”

“I watch a lot of cooking shows and from my mom. She’s an excellent cook.”

“Why don’t I know this about you?”

“I’m a man of mystery.” He dressed his plate and sat next to her. About to take a fork full of eggs, he stopped. “So, what do you plan on doing today?”

Emma hugged her coffee mug. “Skating is on the agenda. Do you skate?”

“Nope. I never learned. Remember, I was raised in California, then moved to Texas. Not too many wintry days or ice rinks.”

“Would you like to try? I can teach you.”

“Gee. I forgot my skates.” He chuckled.

“Hmmm.” She nodded. Then she pondered his sock-covered feet. “Size Twelve?”

“Twelve and a half.” He glanced at his foot and raised a brow. “What are you up to?”

She smiled and poked him in his good shoulder, then winked. “I never give away my secrets.”

Colin liked her spunk. There were questions he wanted to ask, but the timing was never right. Maybe he’d discover more over the next few days. From the first day he’d met her, she’d intrigued him. If Emma weren’t his employee, he would’ve asked her out during their first conversation despite ending a year-long relationship with his ex-girlfriend Belinda.

She finished eating, and they continued their small talk until he took his last bite.

“I’ll take care of the dishes.” He always tidied up as he cooked, so clean-up was a breeze.

“No. Let me.” She stood. “You cooked. I’ll clean.”

“Not this time.” He picked up their plates and walked over to the sink. He expected a protest, but she sat down on the stool while he loaded the dishwasher.

"How's the shoulder?"

He lifted and rotated his arm in a circle. "Sore, and it's stiff, but I'll survive."

"Maybe you should get in the hot tub later today. That might help reduce the soreness. Did you ice all night?"

"I did as you instructed. I even refilled the bag around two o'clock." He'd seen the light under her door and had the urge to knock, but he'd managed to control his momentary lapse in judgment.

"I noticed your light was still on." He gave the counters a quick wipe down.

The entire time, Emma sat at the counter with her chin supported in her hands, watching. "I was on the phone with Georgia just before I let you have it. I promised I call her back."

"How is she?"

"She's Georgia, but she did report Margaret is behaving herself."

Colin shook his head as disappointment rushed in. Margaret wasn't going to make his job easy. He filled their coffee cups, added the extra ingredients, and handed one to Emma.

"I'm impressed. That was a good breakfast."

"You should be. I'm an impressive guy and you're not the only one with organizational skills."

She took the cup and tilted her head. "Boy, you're feisty this morning."

Her cute nose scrunched. He adored her facial expressions, especially her laugh. For months after he started working with Emma, she carried a sadness that controlled her. Her ex had to have done a number on her. He'd always wondered what the entire story was behind the divorce, but that was one of those questions you don't ask in the office or when having fun at Saturday sales.

"Don't drink your coffee yet. Put your coat on." He'd hung their coats on the backs of the dining table chairs. She did as he asked.

"Come on." He motioned for her to follow and headed for the French doors that led to the deck. Before breakfast, in front of the fire pit, he'd placed two Adirondack chairs and spread blankets over them, then started a fire. "Have a seat while I feed the fire."

"What time did you get up?"

"My usual time. Six or so."

She settled into her chair and wrapped herself in the blanket. From behind, he tugged at the edge of the wool fabric and pulled it over her shoulders and the back of her head. Making her happy was the only thing on his agenda for the next four days. "Covering your head will conserve your body temp. Comfy?"

"Very." She snuggled down into the chair.

He sat down next to her in the other Adirondack.

"Aren't you going to cover up your head to conserve your body heat?" Her tone carried a hint of sarcasm.

Colin held up a finger. From under his seat, he pulled out a leather aviator hat, lined in tan fur with flaps that covered his ears. "This should do fine."

Emma burst out in a gut-wrenching laugh that took several seconds for her to control. "Where on earth did you find that?"

"The downstairs storeroom. The Pendletons keep a stash of seasonal clothes in there." He fumbled around under his seat and pulled out a second hat. "I found one for you, too."

Emma threw her head back and continued to laugh. After a few seconds, she composed herself and focused on Colin and his silly hat. She snorted, once again working to control her laughter. Her face glowed and her eyes sparkled, but her laughter warmed him.

"Give me that thing." She lowered the blanket and put the hat on, tilting her head with her hand under her chin. "Model worthy?"

Colin laughed and gave his head a shake. "Not quite."

Emma's mouth never lost its upward tilt as she sipped her coffee. Her laughter pleased him because he'd never seen her laugh so freely. He leaned back in his chair, satisfied with his scenario's effect.

They watched the mountain range change colors from deep purple to shades of blue as the sun moved across the morning sky. In silence, they sipped their coffee with their silly but warm headgear.

Colin watched Emma, whose gaze stayed fixed on the view. Ah, she was relaxing. If only their situations were different, he could become accustomed to having her in his life full-time.

CHAPTER 17

COLIN AND EMMA sat and enjoyed each other's company until the sun passed over the lodge, casting full sunlight on the deck. It marked Emma's signal to hit the ice.

"I'll be right back." Emma dashed downstairs to the backdoor cubbies. Colin wasn't the only one who had an idea of where the Pendletons had stashed extra gear. She'd conducted a semi-snoop before he arrived.

On her knees, she flipped the lid on the first bench and dove into a search to find a pair of skates in Colin's size. She rummaged and pulled out pair after pair until she emptied the bin into a pile next to her. Then she attacked the second. The skate gods shone down on her, the first black pair she pulled out read size 13. Half size larger to make room for bulky socks. "There you are. You'll do nicely."

She wasted no time shoving the pile of skates back into their home. Thank heavens the skates had the laces tied to their mates which made the task easier.

She grabbed her skates, and returned to the deck, to dangle the black pair in front of Colin. "Here you go. Try them on."

A ray of sunlight bounced off the metallic blades and reflected across Colin's face. He reached to lower Emma's hand to clear his vision. "Ice skates."

"Yep. We're going ice skating."

"I don't think so."

Emma dropped her shoulders and pushed out her lower lip. "Come on. What else do you have to do?"

He twisted his mouth and raised a finger to his chin. "I could read." He thumbed over his shoulder. "Did you see the books in this place? I think I might find a sci-fi or war novel that I can finish before we leave."

"Colin." She motioned for him to take the skates. "My arm is getting tired."

He let out a huff, and she swore he rolled his eyes.

"Now you stop." He couldn't resist the way her eyes hugged him. He grabbed the skates and put them on. "What if I fall and break something? We can't get any help up here. How would you even get me back inside? I might freeze to death. Besides, if I fall, I have further to hit the ground." He gestured at her. "You have short legs. Nice legs, but shorter."

She ignored his comment concerning an emergency because she withheld telling him the police chief offered to helicopter them out if they needed help. They had food and water, the lodge was off the grid and Charlie had given her the manual. He walked her through how to check the solar panel, pumps, and whatnot before he left. If she couldn't handle something, he was a phone call away.

Why bother the police when they had his hands full? Maybe she'd never have a romantic future with Colin, but she didn't know when she'd have an opportunity to be alone with him like this, again. She planned to do nothing to mess up their time together.

He stuck his leg out. "They fit. Now what? We walk down the stairs in these?" He nudged toward the outside steps. "That might be risky. Remember, I have more space between me and the ground. Stairs are even scarier. I don't like that idea."

She giggled. "No, silly. Take them off. We'll take our cups in and use the door downstairs. There's a bench along the lake. We'll put them on there."

Once they'd trudged to the lake, Colin studied the deck. "Where were you the day I arrived?"

"Best I can figure, I was sitting right here." She pointed to the bench.

"Makes sense. You can't see it from the windows. The edge of the deck hides it."

She stood next to him and followed his line of sight. "Yep, you're right."

She grinned and gave him an elbow to the ribs. "Stop stalling. Skates on."

Colin huffed. "You're going to make me do this?"

She placed her hands on her hips, straightened, and raised her brows. "Colin Brockman."

Oh, dang. Em pulled the full name thing, just like his mom did when he'd tested her limits. He sat and put on the skates. "All done."

"Let me check the laces. You don't want them too loose." She knelt in the snow and inspected each skate.

Even with that goofy hat, no makeup, and baggy clothes, she was beautiful.

She raised her head. From the cold, her cheeks glowed pink against her pale face. All he'd have to do is raise his hand to run the back of his fingers against her soft skin. Instead, he tucked them into his jacket pockets. After a pat on his ankle, she stood. "They're good."

"Now what?"

"You stand up. Walking in the snow won't be hard." She made a pumping motion with her hands. "Stand."

Colin stood. She took his hand, and they walked to the edge of the lake. She told the truth. Walking on snow was a snap.

"You need to learn a few basics. Watch me." Emma did an about-face and walked across the ice in marching mode. She skated back. "Okay, your turn. Give me your hands. Step onto the ice and stand still for a moment."

Blood surged through his veins. He always avoided making a fool of himself. This time, he had no choice. He almost jumped out of his skin before Emma took his hands. In two steps, he made his way to the slick surface and stood as she instructed.

"Now, we march in place like this." She lifted one foot at a time.

He followed suit.

"Great. Now we march and move just like walking. Hang on to my hands." She led him onto the ice.

"Take off your gloves."

"Why."

"Just do it."

He shoved his leather gloves into his pockets.

"Good. Stand there." She turned and flipped up the tail of her jacket and sweater. "Put your hands on my lower back."

He stared at her well-formed butt clad in the tight-fitting leggings. He rubbed the back of his neck and then held his hands out, not sure where they needed to land. Did she know what this would do to him? "Wait. What?"

"Oh, for heaven's sake." In one fluid motion, as if by instinct, she latched onto his wrists and planted his palms on her lower backside. She didn't let go and started marching. "These are the muscles you use. Can you feel the ones I tighten?"

"Yes, I can." *Oooh, yeah.* He experienced every contracting fibrous strand of her derriere. She had to be trying to kill him. His mouth dried, and he licked his lips until he caught himself. The lip-licking might appear creepy if she noticed. He tightened his lips instead.

"You're doing great. Follow me."

She marched further on the ice and he followed. Hands on her ass the whole time, certain parts of him jumped along with his ticker in his chest.

"I'm going to face you. Don't stop."

Thank God. At least his hands were off her rear. He had less than two seconds to get his act together. He curved the corners of his mouth up as she faced him. "How am I doing?"

"Really well. A few more basics and we'll see how you do on your own."

Emma showed him the proper way to fall and get back up. Falling was easier than he expected and not painful. They practiced something she called squiggles.

The entire time, he never lost his balance and followed along. His daily physical workouts gave him the stamina needed and once he figured out what muscles to use, this skating thing came easy. At least moving forward.

Hand-in-hand, the pair glided over the entire area Charlie had shoveled before they arrived. Emma broke away a few times and made some fancy spins.

Each time an expression of contentment spread across her face. He loved watching her as she glided across the ice and could grow use to seeing her in her element for the rest of his life.

After her last spin, she skated toward him and stopped inches in front of him. "We've been out here for over two hours. The sun is setting. You ready to go in?"

"Yep." Colin attempted to start to skate, but something went wrong. He plowed right into her. Without thinking, and not knowing how he pulled off his next move, he wrapped his arms around her and twisted. When they hit the ice, she lay on top of him, nose to nose. For him, moments turned into years as they stared into each other's eyes. Then he spoke, "Are you okay?"

"I think so."

Her quick breaths skimmed his face. He watched the pupils of her chocolate-colored eyes dilate. Under the weight of his arms, her muscles tensed. All he had to do was lift his head and touch his lips to hers.

Emma blinked. "I'm getting hungry."

"Should we make an early dinner?" He finished with, "And maybe a movie."

CHAPTER 18

THE MOVIE ENDED around 9:30 p.m. What had possessed him to agree to watch a romance? He rubbed his thumb and forefinger from the outer edges of his lids to the bridge of his nose to swipe away the watery film.

Emma curled up on the other end of the loveseat, her feet tucked under her. A few times he noticed her wipe her cheeks.

"I'm glad you talked me into watching that movie." He lied like a skier, telling himself he'd stop before smacking that tree dead in his path. "Can I ask you something?" A question nagged at him for nine months because he waited for her to tell him, but she never did. He didn't know if she'd answer, but he figured what the heck.

"I guess so."

"What were you doing sleeping on the couch in my office?" He'd waited for the answer. His palms moistened and his foot resting across his knee bounced in a steady rhythm.

She bit her lower lip, then parted her mouth. "What you're talking about."

"The night before my first day. You gave me an excuse I never bought."

Dryness filled his mouth, and he hoped he hadn't forced a conversational shutdown.

She squirmed and pulled her legs closer to her. "Oh, yeah. I told you I worked late and figured I'd stretch out to rest for a few minutes. Then I guess I fell asleep."

He raised a palm toward her. "You don't need to say anything else if you don't want to, but the next day, I noticed you'd only changed your blouse."

She tucked her chin but glanced in his direction. One side of her mouth quirked upward. "And noticed it was unbuttoned."

He shrugged one shoulder. "Yeah. Can't blame a guy for that."

"You scared the crap out of me when I woke up with Jan's throw over me."

"You looked cold." *And like an angel sleeping.* He sat back against the loveseat and remained quiet to give her space. She'd either stop talking or open up. He prayed for the latter.

She took in a long inhalation and then let the air out slowly before she spoke. "I was homeless and had been living in your office for two weeks."

"What!?" He repositioned himself to face her.

"My divorce was not very civil. We were still living together. I was short on funds." She pursed her lips. "Your office offered me an inexpensive and private place to sleep for a few weeks."

He studied her, speechless.

She shut up and coiled into a tighter ball.

He searched his brain for something that wouldn't make him sound like a total idiot. He came up empty, but her next statement floored him.

"I was married to Benedict Corban."

Colin shot into a straighter position. "The Benedict Corban who's the youngest son of the Toronto Corbans."

Her body contracted more and her voice muted, "Yes, that's the one."

"Gee. I met that guy at one of the company events. He didn't impress me much."

Emma swung her head toward Colin. "I agree. Most people wouldn't admit that because of who he is." She wrapped a hand around her outer ankle and pulled her leg closer.

If she continued to retract, Colin suspected she'd disappear into the arm of the loveseat.

"Most people think I was nuts to divorce him."

"Care to tell me about it?" He craved to discover her story.

She repositioned herself to sit with her arms wrapped around her knees, which she drew close to her upper body. Then she wasted no time.

"We met at university and he swept me off my feet. Before graduation, he asked me to marry him. Of course, I had to sign a prenup, but I was young and crazy in love. And like a fool, I didn't read it. Nor did I realize he only needed to be married for his trust fund to kick in, exactly two years after our wedding." Her stare remained fixed on an invisible object somewhere on the wall.

She reached for her glass of wine and took a sip. "Soon after we came back from our honeymoon, the trouble started." She filled him in on the nasty details. "The insults became harsher and his words were crueler. He loved telling me how stupid I was."

Colin watched her jaw clench. "Emma, did he ever hit you?"

She shook her head. "No. He came close during a few of his rages but never did. I later found out that if he physically laid hands on me, he took the risk of losing his money as part of the prenup. Instead, he used psychological and economic abuse."

A tear ran down her cheek and one quick swipe made it disappear. "He put me on a strict allowance. I had to beg him for money just for the basics to run the house. Then he called me stupid for not managing money the right way." She expressed a sigh and again wiped at an escaping tear.

Colin raked his fingers through his hair and shook his head. "The guy's an ass. You're the smartest woman I know."

"Thank you." She tucked her chin as she fingered her pant leg. "When he flaunted his mistress in front of me, I'd had enough. I gave up a boatload of money and divorced the creep."

"Sounds like you made the right decision."

"It's taken multiple visits to a therapist to figure that out and..." She raised her wine glass. "...and a bunch of this." She took a sip.

"What about your family?"

"My mom and dad died when I was in sixth grade. Car crash."

Colin watched the sadness he'd witnessed so often wash over her face. "That must've been tough."

"Before they died, they were never around much. Always busy with work or some social event. I spent a lot of time at Georgia's. Her family became my family." She touched her glass to her lips and then added, "Georgia talked her parents into taking me in. They became my foster parents and prevented me from taking a nose dive into the system."

"I see." *What kind of response was that*? But again he said nothing and was glad she kept talking.

"I guess when I married Benedict I wanted someone to save me." She huffed. "Boy, was I wrong. He did the opposite. He destroyed me, and I let him."

"How can you say that? You left him."

"I should've read the prenup. That document would've clued me in. But I didn't. I trusted him." She shook her head. "Instead, I kept telling myself things would get better."

"But you did get out."

"Eventually."

He had doubts about asking his next question, but she was sharing her life with him and if she didn't want to answer, she'd tell him. "This is changing the subject, but do you like working with me?"

Her eyes widened, and her head moved back. Then she uncoiled for the first time since they sat down. She no longer hugged her legs and repositioned herself to face him. Her posture, open and relaxed.

She rested her arm on the back of the couch, her hand close to his shoulder, and then she fiddled with the seam of his shirt sleeve. "I love working with you." She gave him a tap. "You're my work-husband."

A burst of adrenaline pushed through his veins. She used the words husband and love almost together. Maybe he did have a chance if his plan to fire Margaret worked. Emma could slip into that director position and as two employees in management, no rules would be broken if they dated or even married.

That made him smile, and he gave a muffled chuckle. "And you're my work-wife, but that title obligates you to like working with me. Although you might be the only one at this point." He made a point not to repeat the word love.

That might've been a slip on her part. She called him her work-husband. He thought of her that way and, funny, she had similar thoughts.

Emma understood the hurt that brushed over Colin's face. After spending time with him, she realized that in his soul, he wanted to do a good job. "I told you my story. What's yours?"

"Should I start with Belinda dumping me for my best friend, or why I'm the most dreaded boss in history?"

"Tsk. You're not an awful boss. Besides, I know the answer to that." She rubbed the top of his shoulder. "This retreat can change all that. Besides, Georgia likes you." No, Georgia crushed on Colin and told Emma at every opportunity just how much.

"Well, I like Georgia, too."

With her right index finger, she pointed up as she spoke. "Are you talking about the Belinda that you talk to all the time?"

His brows knitted, and he squinted. He jumped over her question. "This retreat has to be so uncomfortable for Margaret so her icy facade snaps."

Enough with the office talk. She wanted the skinny on his heartbreak. "If the van gets here, the office part will take care of itself. Now, tell me about Belinda." His shoulder got another tap before she adjusted her position to get the whole story.

His hand swiped his chin. "About two years ago, I met her at the Pendleton's New Year's Eve party. We dated for about a year and I asked her to move to Canada. She never agreed because she was in love with Robert—"

"Robert Pendleton?"

"Yeah. My best friend and son of the big boss Robert aka Rob Pendleton."

She giggled. "What is it with that family and their need to name everyone Robert?"

"I know. That confused the heck out of me at first, too." He raised his gaze. "Should I continue?"

"Yes." Of course, she wanted every little detail.

He proceeded and tell Emma the story of how Belinda had a car accident and was in a coma for six months. While in the coma she dreamt she met, fell in love with, and married Robert. When she woke up, she still loved Robert and realized he didn't exist because he was a dream.

"Literally, the man of her dreams." She placed a hand over her heart and patted her chest. She fantasized about his tale of lost love, and it almost made her cry.

"I guess you could say that. Anyway, she met him at the New Year's Eve party. Then things got very interesting."

"Did she and Robert recognize each other?"

"Yep, they did, and that's the strange part. She knew him right off the bat, but Robert was engaged and told no one he recognized her. So, both kept their distance. She refused to be the other woman and backed off. He'd made a commitment to Sharyn, his fiancée, that he was determined to keep. So they became friends when she started working for his mom." Colin attempted to pour himself another glass. "Bottle's empty. I'll be right back."

"Hurry. I want to know how this ends." Emma bounced in her seat. This was better than any romance movie.

The crackle of the fire commanded her attention. The quietness of the room, the heat from the flames, and the excellent wine tranquilized her mind. Her lids grew heavy. She laid her head against the back of the loveseat and if Colin took much longer, she'd be asleep.

The thump of footsteps down the stairs produced Colin with full hands.

"Sorry, I took so long. I put together a charcuterie board and brought this." He held out a bottle of bourbon. He placed the mini feast and the bottle on the table in front of the overstuffed loveseat they'd nestled in during the movie.

"More food? At this rate, I'll have a postal code named after me."

"And a pretty postal code it'd be. Your bourbon." He held out a glass. "Enjoy. Besides, you'll skate the calories off. There's a lot of muscle action going on there." He slathered a cracker with cheese spread and stuffed it in his mouth.

At least her plans to get tipsy might come to fruition, but she'd have to keep herself in check. Even though they were telling their secrets, he was her boss.

His sense of humor intensified away from the office. He was different, less stuffy, and more easy-going. She always enjoyed seeing this side of him and longed for more. "Hurry up and chew. I want more of the story."

"Okay. Okay," he muttered through his mouth full of food just before he swallowed. "Well, Robert broke up with his fiancée. No, Sharyn threw the ring at him and told him to get his stuff out of her apartment. The rest was history."

"Wait, are you telling me Robert and Belinda just hooked up and didn't give you a second thought?"

He waved his hands. "No. No. When I asked her to move to Canada, she explained her coma dream and said she'd always loved Robert. I gave both of them permission to move on because..." His gaze drifted toward the licking flames. "On some level, I knew I'd never make it past the friend stage with her."

His intense expression tugged at her soul. She placed her hand on his arm. "Colin, didn't that hurt?"

He filled his lungs, then let out a sigh. "At first, then I saw how happy they were and knew they were meant to be together." He leaned in closer. "How could I be mad about that?"

Her heart hiccupped. She laid her hand over her chest. "Are you telling me they found their 'happily ever after'?"

He thinned his lips and nodded "That's exactly what I'm saying." He nudged her arm and winked. "So, kid, there's hope for us yet."

She cocked a brow. *Was he talking about them getting together? No. That couldn't happen. Or could it?* Her next question might've been out of line, but she asked anyway. "Are you talking about us dating?"

He swung his head at lightning speed in her direction, his brow furrowed. "Ah. No. Um, I meant us finding our own someone to love."

He drifted his line of sight forward and swallowed hard. A serious expression overcame his face. He took a few seconds and then uttered his next statement, which made her wish she had a hole to disappear into.

"Would *us* getting together be a bad thing?"

She wanted to scream, "*No.*" Of course, she longed to explore a romantic relationship with the sweetest and sexiest man she'd ever met. She fantasized about it, but a fantasy is all that could materialize. She'd made a vow that she'd never trust a rich guy again and she was sticking to her decision.

She attempted a political retort. "First, there's the corporate fraternization policy. Next, we come from two different sides of the track, me from the shanty and you from the mansions. Our worlds would collide."

"Wait. Do you think my family has money?"

"Don't you? You live in a pricy high-rise, drive a luxury car, have expensive taste in clothes, and hang with rich folks." She raised her hands, palms up, to refer to his relationship with the Pendletons as she scanned the room full of leather loveseats arranged in neat, tiered rows. "I assumed."

"You assumed wrong. It's quite the opposite."

CHAPTER 19

COLIN WATCHED EMMA'S face brighten to a bright pink flush as she brushed her palms over her thighs. "I'm sorry."

He offered her a cracker with the cheesy spread. "That's okay. That's why this retreat has to work. There's too much riding on the results."

She relaxed and twisted to face him. "Tell me more." Other than meeting his mother, he had shared very little about his past.

He slouched into the leather back of the loveseat and filled his lungs. "I was born on a snowy, sub-zero night. My mother hopped into a cab and almost had me in the back seat."

He snuck a quick peek to see Emma squint and her mouth twist. He continued. "About to pop out, the driver stopped to assist."

"Colin, are you pulling my leg?"

He let out a hardy laugh. "I was wondering when you'd catch on and stop me."

She poked his arm. "Get serious."

"Hey, that hurt." He pointed to his shoulder. "Bruise."

She tapped her finger against her cheek to scrutinize his shoulder. "Oh, stop. Besides, it's your other arm."

He grunted. "By the way, you were right. I sat in the hot tub before you got up and that helped." He moved the arm in a circular motion. "See. Much better."

She cocked her head. "Good. I'll hit that side next time."

"What, no pity?"

"Your story."

"All right." He tapped the arm of the loveseat. This next part struck a nerve. "I never knew my father. He was killed outside our apartment when I was about five months old. Some guy jumped and stabbed him for his wallet. He died before anyone even knew he was lying in the street."

"Oh, my gosh. That's horrible." She laid her hand over his. The warmth she generated comforted him.

When the words came out of his mouth, he fought to keep the tears back. A knot formed in his stomach. He couldn't tell if the touch of Emma's gentle hand caused his breathing to cease or if he had never before shared this story with anyone.

A lump formed in his throat. He forced himself to continue. "Mom got his life insurance, but it wasn't much. She had to find a job, and fast, to support us."

Talking became more difficult between the dry swallows. He needed a break. "Excuse me. I'll be right back." He thumbed over his shoulder. "Bathroom."

He double-timed it to the half-bath in the game room just past the bar. In the confines of the small space, he planted a palm on the closed door and stroked his face. His mother had given so much to make sure he had everything he needed. She'd worked two jobs, found good childcare, and kept him safe.

With his cupped hands full of cold water, he splashed his face. Then he checked for signs of sentimentality and eye redness. One swipe with the hand towel left him satisfied Emma couldn't tell he'd almost cried.

He filled his lungs and took a few minutes to regain control then walked back to Emma.

"Where'd I leave off?" He plopped onto the loveseat. The leather squeaked on contact.

"Your mom had to find work."

"She did everything she could to make sure I had what I needed." He raised a hand and gave a slight wave. "I never knew we were poor until I reached college. College was an eye-opener. There was an entire world I never knew about and one I couldn't afford. On breaks, I'd worked to help pay for my education." He took a drawn-out breath and let out the air as slowly as he took it in. "Most of my classmates went on expensive vacations."

"Is that why you studied finance?"

"Yeah. I realized if I invested well, that was the best route." He noticed Emma's inquisitive expression. "What?"

"You have nice things and live well minus your lack of furniture." She held up a finger. "Which with my expertise we fixed."

He detected a sneer in her voice, but he smiled. She made him smile. "Not really. I figured out in college that to be successful, you have to look the part. I spend my money wisely. I have a high-end address but no furniture until you helped me out." He paused. "And may I add, saved me a boatload of money."

He grinned. I buy and wear good suits at the office. The rest of the time I live in sweats. I don't eat out. I cook all my meals. Hence, my gourmet cooking skills." He paused again. "The only exception to my savings plan is my car. Sadie is my one spending splurge."

Emma relaxed her arms. "And this works?"

"It's all an illusion and I had you fooled."

"Why this intense need to save?" She stared at him.

Her inquisition took him by surprise, but he continued. "My parents had nothing when my father died. If I ever get married and my family finds themselves in the same position, they will be comfortable."

Emma's face softened. "I see. And what about your mother?"

"I send her money every month and she's enjoying her golden years in California. I tried to get her to move to Toronto, but she hates the cold. She usually visits twice during the warm months, and I fly to see her in the winter. We Zoom at least once a week."

His thoughts drifted to the first woman he ever loved. The one who raised him and one to whom he owed everything.

Emma studied Colin. The light from the fire cast shadows over the shallow crevices of his noble face. The shading appeared as deep sadness. She reached to touch his arm. "Colin."

He shook his head. "I'm sorry. Must be the bourbon making me moody."

"Or the fact that you love your mother."

His icy blues locked onto hers. Her respirations quickened. There was so much more to this man than she'd ever given him credit for. His life story made hers appear shallow in comparison.

An image of Colin sitting in a webbed aluminum chair with his long legs almost to his chin raced into her mind as she took a sip of bourbon. The honey-colored liquor spurted out of her mouth and nose at the same time she laughed. She reached for a napkin to wipe her mouth and clean up the mess. "Sorry. The image of you relaxing in a lawn chairs was too much."

"Glad I amuse you. But what are you talking about?"

She grinned. "The lawn chairs you had before we did your place. It makes me laugh, thinking of you sitting in one. You'd never fit. You're too long."

He rubbed his mouth. "I was, wasn't I? I have to admit the couch is much more comfortable."

She nodded. "I'm glad I helped you out of your misery."

"We did good." Their moment only lasted a second. He slapped his hands on his thighs. "Time for a game of pool."

"I don't know how to play." She dabbed at her mouth and then crunched the napkin.

"I took a skating lesson from you all afternoon. Now, it's your turn to learn how to play pool." He snapped to his feet, took her hand, and tugged her up.

In an instant, she stood, inches from his warm body. Her nether parts twitched. *Get a grip, girl.*

"Let's take this with us." He handed her the bottle of bourbon and their glasses. Then he picked up their snacks. At the door, he flipped off the lights.

"Let's put everything on the bar." He walked over to the pool cues and selected one for Emma. After a few basic instructions, he racked up the balls she'd scattered over the table earlier. "Ladies first."

She leaned over the table, held the cue stick as Colin had instructed, and poked at the white ball, which did very little to spread out the other balls. Rolling the cue ball by hand yesterday was much easier than using the stupid stick.

Colin wrapped his hands around his cue with the rubber end resting on his foot. "Okay."

"Pretty bad?"

"Give it a few more tries." He walked over to the table and explained his movements as he sent the white Bakelite projectile slamming into the cluster. The sound of Bakelite hitting Bakelite permeated the room as the balls slammed against one another and shot in all directions over the felt surface. He sank two solid-colored balls. "Your turn."

"Now, I'm stripes, right?"

"That's right. You have several choices." He pointed his cue to the striped balls closest to the cue ball and in a direct line to a pocket. "Just take your time, aim, and shoot."

That little white bugger just grazed the striped ball with her failed attempt. "What am I doing wrong?" She held her stick to her side and coated the tip with chalk. Like that might help. She glared at Colin. "Hey, some help here."

"Oh. Right." He walked to her side. "Lean over the table and set your cue stick on your fingers."

She followed his instructions. "Now what?"

What he did next, she wasn't prepared for.

Colin leaned over and pressed against her back. He then reached over to her hand holding the stick. He wrapped her other hand with his free one. The heat from his body engulfed every inch of her. His scent of fresh soap and a trace of his leather-citrus cologne enticed her nose. *Was that lavender? She inhaled deeper. It was lavender, and she loved lavender. Did he use lavender soap?*

He whispered the instructions into her ear, and her feminine parts tingled. A staccato beat hammered in her ears. She didn't hear a word he said.

"Okay, ready." Still draped around her, he plunged the cue forward and sank a striped ball. "And that's how it's done."

How was what done? She moved her head to the left and found Colin centimeters from her face. His breath warmed her lips. *OMG.* "I think I've had enough for one night."

Colin released his hold and stood.

She glanced at the clock above the bar. "It's 1:30. I need to get to sleep."

"At least let me walk you home."

She stood and stepped far enough away to ignore his manly impact on her. "Walk me home?"

"To your door."

She snickered at his absurd idea, but what did she have to lose? Her job—if there was more on his mind than there was on hers. "If you insist."

Colin shelved the bourbon before they carried their leftovers to the kitchen. "I'll take care of this in the morning." He started for the stair to the bedroom level.

"Hey. Remember, I'm down here." She pointed to the hallway that led to her bedroom. He studied her in a captivating way and his stare stirred those giddy feelings all over again.

"Yeah, I remember." He stretched out his hand in the hall's direction and motioned for her to go first. "Why did you decide to change rooms?"

"It'll be quieter for me once the retreat starts."

"If it starts."

"Keep your fingers crossed." She began to walk. What on earth was she thinking? Letting him walk her home. This meant trouble if he had any ideas. Would she stop him, if he tried? That was the big question. She had to admit to herself that saying "no" might be hard.

At the door, she stood in front of him and thumbed toward the room. "This is me."

"Emma, thank you."

"For what?"

"Today. I had a nice time."

She smiled. "We have at least three more days for nice times."

"I'll look forward to them."

A few awkward seconds passed, yet they both stood their ground. She tilted her head. “Is there something else?”

He shoved his hands in his front pockets and rocked back on his heels. “I need to make sure you’re safe in your room. It’s Bro code.”

“Oh. I forgot.” She reached for the knob, opened the door, and walked in. From inside, she gave Colin one last glimpse. “See. Safe inside. Good night.” And with that, she closed the door.

In the dark, she leaned her forehead against the back of the door. *What am I doing?*

CHAPTER 20

EMMA TOSSED AND turned. She had intermittent dreams about a huge field of lavender with Colin standing in the center. Around 2:00 a.m. she awoke. She left her room and walked down the hall to the carved wooden staircase. She stood for a moment, barefoot and wearing only her shorty pajamas. She listened in the darkness then, placed one foot on the bottom stair step, and hesitated. *Dare I do this*?

If she ascended the steps and walked down the hall, she'd be in front of his door. One knock, he'd answer, and there'd be no coming back from that decision.

Blood pounded in her ears. She tightened her grip on the rail, took another step, and stopped.

She realized that as much as she wanted, she couldn't cross his bedroom's threshold. If she decided to follow her instinct, there worlds would change forever.

Her lids lowered. For a moment she pictured his face when he opened the door to invite her in and how he'd sweep her off her feet. Twinges of sexual awareness raced through every inch of her body. Then, she let her shoulders drop before walking back to her room. Sleep didn't come easy.

The room filled with the morning sun. Emma pulled a cotton-covered pillow over her face. From under its corner, she peeked at the clock on the bedside table—11 a.m. An hour later than yesterday. If she kept this up, getting back to her daily work routine might have some challenges.

She flung the pillow to the other side of the king bed and stretched. She needed coffee. Her feet touched the floor, and she padded to the bathroom to get ready for the day.

Dressed, Emma walked out of the bathroom and she noticed a piece of paper with uneven edges near the bottom of the bedroom door. She picked it up and unfolded it to reveal a paper snowflake. In the middle was a handwritten note: *Meet me in the great room. I have a surprise.* The corners of her mouth spread upward. Tiny jitters spread in her stomach, amused by how all their notes were on paper snowflakes. She forgot her quest for coffee and placed the snowflake on the nightstand. She darted out the door to see what was so important.

Moments later, she found Colin standing in front of a ten-foot spruce placed next to the fireplace covered in white lights. Her hand covered her mouth, and her spirits brightened. She loved Christmas. Planning for the retreat had taken her away from her own Christmas decorating, and Colin's tree made a great substitute.

A coffee mug in Colin's hand appeared in front of her. "You like?" He motioned toward the tree.

She took the mug. "Where did you get it?"

He positioned his shoulders sideways so she'd see his blank expression. She giggled. "Right. The woods."

"Yep. I could've cut down a bigger one, but then I'd have trouble getting it in here and standing it up by myself."

"I would've helped."

"I know, but I wanted to surprise you. Did I?"

"Yes, you did. Where'd you get the lights and stand?" She glanced at the thoughtful man standing next to her. Maybe she could get more intimate with him. She shook her head to rid herself of the thought. If she did that, she'd jeopardize Emma's Attic and her dream. Instead, she sipped her coffee.

"The lights were in the garage and I made the stand from some scraps I found in the firewood bin."

"Colin, it's beautiful. Are there any decorations around here?"

He crossed his arms across his chest. "Nah, I called Robert, and he told me there was never a need since the family didn't come up here for Christmas. He said I'd find the lights in the garage and that his mom strung them on the deck during their fishing trips.

"It is a little bare."

"Got any ideas?"

She set her cup down on a side table. "I do have an idea." She disappeared into the study and went straight to the closet, where she had seen several reams of printer paper. She grabbed a pack, then rummaged through the drawers and found a package of glue sticks, a bottle of glue, and all things, silver glitter. Next, she picked up a stapler, two pairs of scissors, and the tape dispenser from the top of the mahogany desk. Arms full, she walked into the great room and placed her supplies on the coffee table.

"What's all this?"

"Our evening's entertainment."

"Arts and crafts?" He poked through the pile.

She picked up her mug. "Sort of. Didn't you ever make paper chains? And I know you can make paper snowflakes. By the way, thank you."

One nod gave his acknowledgment.

Despite all the times she spent alone as a kid at Christmas, she still loved this time of the year—what the holiday represented. Christmas helped her renew her faith that her plans had meaning and that she'd be okay.

He gave her a gentle nudge with his elbow. "I like it. Let's eat breakfast." He checked his watch and cocked a brow at Emma. "Maybe we should have lunch?"

She wrinkled her nose. "Give me a break. I'm on vacation."

"Come on." He clasped her arm to lead her into the kitchen. "Let's get you another cup of coffee."

"After breakfast… I mean lunch." She leaned against the counter. "I want to skate for a few hours. Will you come with me?"

"I thought you'd never ask."

She stopped in mid-stride and shoved her coffee mug into his hands.

"I'll be right back."

"Where're you going?"

"This won't take long."

"Okay. I guess I'll wait here in the kitchen."

She grabbed her coat and raced down the path to the garage. Inside she peeked in several boxes until she found what she wanted.

"There you are." She picked up a box and scanned a shelf full of spray paint. "You'll do nicely." With a swooped up a can of red paint.

Back in the house, she placed the box on the kitchen counter.

"What's this?" Colin reduced the heat on the burner and walked over to her.

"More decorations. I saw these when I pulled my car into the garage. There's got to be about twenty to thirty pinecones in here." She picked up the paint can. "We spray them before we go skating and let them dry. Add some glue to the tips, dip them in the glitter, and we have tree ornaments."

"I like that idea." He picked one up and rotated it from side to side. "They're huge."

"And perfect. But what do we use to hang them and the snowflakes?" She knitted her brows.

Colin tapped her nose. "I've got that covered, Little Lady. Fishing line. There's a ton in the storeroom." He checked the clock on the stove. "We've got a busy day ahead of us if we plan on skating and decorating that tree. Let's eat."

She propped herself on a stool and watched Colin finish preparing a delicious breakfast or lunch, whatever he wanted to call it. He had her in awe. Underneath that portentous exterior was a sweet and considerate man. He was husband material for some lucky woman. Who knows? Maybe sometime in the future, she'd be lucky to find someone like him when she got her life together. Too bad her timing was off and that time wasn't now.

Colin sat on the lake bench and watched Emma come out of a spin. Confidence dripped off her, exhibited by her command of grace and the ease at which she skated. He found it difficult to believe that less than a year ago, she'd lost all sense of herself because of her abusive husband.

She skated toward him. Her face flushed and her mouth curved into a huge smile. The grind of ice against her skate's toe pick brought her to a halt in front of him.

"I could watch you do that all day."

He stood, wrapped a towel around her neck, and held on to the ends. Their gaze met. His pulse pounded. He tilted his head, pulled at the towel, and moved in closer to her mouth.

Her eyes widened. She stepped back and dabbed the beads of sweat from her forehead. "Do what?"

He shifted his weight and cleared his throat, realizing he pushed too close to that fraternization line. "Skate. You're good. Did you ever think about going pro?"

She laughed. "I'm not good enough."

A glance at her face told him they needed to move on from his thoughtless attempt to kiss her.

"What time is it?"

He checked his watch. "Three."

"Let's go in and get started. We have a tree to decorate."

After they stowed their skates, Colin followed Emma to the kitchen. She headed for the table where they left the painted pinecones spread out on newspaper and touched several. "They're dry." She picked one up and studied it. "Perfect—you added the right amount of color." Pinecone in hand, she regarded him. "Good job, Mr. Brockman."

He realized his stunt with the towel made her uncomfortable. As long as he maintained a safe distance, he'd have a handle on his emotions. He gave one distinctive bend of the waist. "As long as no one thinks something died from the red paint stains in the snow outside. Kinda grisly."

She laughed. "I'm sure. How about we start with the chain? That will take the longest to make."

He pointed to the great room. "At the coffee table."

"Yep."

"I'll get the paper cutter from the study."

"And I'll make some hot chocolate."

He gave her a thumbs-up as he walked away. He was enjoying himself for the first time since he moved to Canada, even more than their weekend sales. The closeness to Emma made him wish the team would never arrive and the two of them could stay in the lodge forever. He imagined a life with her away from work—one where they lived together and loved.

She stood at the stove, stirring when he walked in with the paper cutter tucked under his arm. He cleared a section of her earlier deposits on the coffee table and set it down.

"What do you think? One or two inches wide for the chain."

She'd poured the cocoa into red and green striped mugs. "At least two and cut down the eleven-inch side. The tree can take a big chain, and the longer loops means less work for us." She picked up the mugs and stopped. "Hey. You want marshmallows?"

"Of course. What's hot cocoa without marshmallows."

Colin dove into the task of cutting strips. A few minutes later, Emma placed his mug on the side table closest to him and hers on the other. She started joining loops while Colin continued to cut. Once he had a pile of strips, he picked up a stapler and followed her lead, but from the opposite end. As a team, they finished about thirty feet or nine meters in forty-five minutes.

"I'll go get the step stool. We can put up what we've done and see how much more we need." He returned, and the pair worked in tandem to drape the tree. They continued the process with a few more feet of chain. In no time, their handy work draped around the tree.

Colin watched Emma's movements as she stepped back. She gave a little jump on her toes and clapped. The reflection of the tree's white lights twinkled in her eyes. He saw her delight when she sighed and cupped her cheeks.

"It's beautiful. But we're not done yet." She sat on the couch and waved him over to join her. "Come on. We have a bunch of snowflakes to make."

"I will, but first I'll build a fire."

With the last log placed in the fireplace, he stood to see Emma busy folding and cutting different shapes to make varying sizes of snowflakes. The side of his mouth quirked up. Her hair wasn't perfect, she wore no makeup, and in her baggy sweater, she was the opposite of her work attire. He liked this side of her. "How many did you make?"

She picked at three stacks of large, medium, and small snowflakes. "Maybe ten."

"How many do you think we need?

"Let's start with thirty, ten of each size."

"Okay, let's get this finished."

They cut three different sizes and with every snowflake, Colin finished, he added a joke to make her laugh. He loved her laughter.

"I love Christmas. It's a special time of the year." She stopped to study their tree. "I didn't have time to put up my decorations. This is a pleasant substitute. Thank you."

She lifted her face to him. The glow on her features made him want to take her in his arms and kiss her silly. "My pleasure. Mom always made sure we had Christmas, no matter how much she had to work to make it happen." He stopped. "I didn't appreciate what she did for me when I was a kid."

"But you do now and you're doing right by her." She winked. "Keep cutting." As she folded a blank piece of paper she added, "Before my parents died, I'd put the tree up every year. If I didn't, there'd be none. I guess that's why I like decorating. It makes me feel like I belong somewhere." She never diverted her attention from the paper.

That was one of the saddest things Colin had ever heard. Her childhood had to be filled with loneliness. He wanted to embrace her and tell her she did belong, she belonged with him. "But Georgia's family changed that."

"They did. But I was always very aware I was the outsider. Maybe that's why I tried so hard with Benedict." She kept turning and cutting the paper. "I wanted to fit in." She dropped her work to her lap with a vacant stare. "I never did."

He wanted to put his arm around her and pull her close, but couldn't. "Well, you're fitting in nicely right now. And thank you."

"For what?"

"The past two very enjoyable days. Are you enjoying yourself?"

She turned toward him. A broad smile spread across her face. "Yes. Of course." She jetted her chin toward him. "Colin Brockman, keep cutting."

She pulled the double name card again. "Yes, Ma'am." He saluted.

They made quick work of the snowflakes.

"Come on. To the dining table."

Colin picked up the glue. "I'll dab the tips and you sprinkle." They worked over the newspaper-covered table.

"When you're done, please tie on the fishing line."

They sat shoulder to shoulder. Colin wanted to say something, but what? How about they sneak around and start dating? No one at the office would know. Everything he thought of sounded stupid. At a loss, he kept to small talk.

Several times their shoulders bumped, and that sent an unexpected charge through his body. Such physical closeness to Emma had his nerves and passion on edge.

Emma pushed away from the table. "Let's get the pinecones and the snowflakes on the tree so we can judge how many more we need. We'll only decorate the front and sides."

In her element as Commander-in-Chief, he enjoyed watching her take charge. "Fine with me."

Colin stood on the step stool while Emma directed him where to hang a pinecone or a snowflake. She stood back and tilted her head from one side to the next. "It needs a star."

"I have an idea." Colin stepped down and picked up three pieces of kindling, and snapped each so they'd be about the same size. He arranged each piece to cross over one another and meet in the center where he bound the pieces with fishing line. After a quick rummage in a few kitchen drawers, his search produced a roll of tinfoil. He covered the bound sticks with the foil. "Ta-da." He held up a six-pointed star. "Would you like to do the honors?"

His soul soared when his gaze rested on her face with a big smile. The firelight enhanced her features as she took the makeshift star in her hands to study it. At that moment, she was the most beautiful woman in the world.

“I’d love to, but I think this is a job for someone your height.” She handed it back.

He stepped on the stool and used two twist ties he snagged from the kitchen. In seconds, the star was secure.

They stood in front of the tree, scrutinizing their work. He placed his arm over her shoulders and pulled her close. She didn’t stiffen, remained relaxed, and wrapped an arm around his back. “Not bad for two big kids.”

She nuzzled into his side as she studied their handiwork. “We did good. If the team gets here, they’ll be impressed.”

Why did she have to break the spell and bring up the team? “Yeah, the team.” He hugged her shoulder and wished the team never existed.

CHAPTER 21

"LET'S GET THIS mess cleaned up. Afterward, bourbon or wine?" Colin snatched the trash bag and stuffed in the debris.

"I have a better idea. How about a hot toddy in front of our beautiful tree and fire?" Emma wanted to enjoy their creation alone with him. In a couple of days, there'd be a house full of people and their time together would come to an end.

"That sounds great but we need to eat something. I'll get something after I dump the trash."

"I finish up in here." She made quick work of putting everything in its place. With her hands on her hips, she surveyed the room before she headed for the kitchen. As she walked by the stove she turned heat on under the kettle then collected everything else she needed.

Colin closed the back door.

"I saw a bottle of whiskey downstairs. Would you go get it?"

"Sure."

The kettle whistled as Colin came up the stairs. His step brisk, his face relaxed, and no stress showed in his body. The morning soaks in the hot tub helped the stiff shoulder and he reported increased movement daily.

The time off was good for both of them.

"Thank you." She poured a hefty amount of the honey-colored liquor into the waiting insulated mugs, added some honey, and hot water. After a good stir, she plopped in a cinnamon stick.

"I'll have some food together in no time. I'll meet you by the fireplace."

She settled on the couch and held the warm mug. Emma was very aware that from the point of view of the management team, her role as Colin's executive assistant hadn't changed. They'd have no clue about the emotional roller coaster she'd experienced in the past two days—close to the man she'd admired from the first time his glacier blues studied her.

She'd revert to her work position where she'd watch doors close and where she'd, once again, be the outsider looking in. A status she'd never really learned to tolerate, until Colin. Even though he was her boss, he treated her like an equal in the confines of their office.

Colin interrupted her pity party when he place a platter of cheese, salami, crackers, grapes, and sliced pears on the coffee table.

"Here you go."

"Oh that looks good." She munched down a few crackers piled with cheese and salami. "Hmmm. I didn't realize how hungry I was."

"I can go make something more."

"No. A few more of these and some fruit will be enough." She stuffed another cracker in her mouth followed by a pear slice. Not very lady like, but she didn't care. Colin joined in by helping himself.

After they finished off the platter, they sat sipping their drinks in the glow of the Christmas tree lights and the flickering flames in the fireplace. The quiet lasted about ten seconds.

"We need something to cover up the base. I'll be right back." Emma dashed down the hall to the linen closet. She grabbed a white, flat king sheet and returned to the great room. "We can use this." In a few shakes, she unfolded the sheet. "Colin, come help me. We need to spread this out under the tree. Take this corner and start over there." She pointed to the left side.

She got down on her stomach and shifted her sight back at Colin just standing holding one corner of the sheet. "Come on. Get down here."

He followed her lead. "Now what?"

"We crawl under the tree to wrap the sheet around the base."

They moved at the same time on either side of the trunk.

"Ouch." Colin rubbed the top of his head. His broad shoulders filled the space between the lower branches and the floor. "I should have trimmed a few of these off." He lay flat, struggling to progress.

Emma buried her face in the sheet and snickered. Muffled squeaks emerged as she tried to control herself. She rested her head on her arm to find Colin watching her. Those glacier blues intensified with small flecks of teal. Her stomach tightened, and a twitch centered below her navel. When the rest of the group arrived, they'd have to keep their distance from one another and she'd miss him. "We need to finish."

"Right."

The spell broke.

"This is as far as I can go. But..." He stretched out his long arm and pulled the sheet to meet Emma's end.

Their fingertips touched and played. A wave of thrilled emotion jetted through her until she pulled her hand back to break the enchantment, again.

An audible gush escaped his lungs. "Now can I back out?"

"Yes, you can."

He scooted back from under the tree first. As Emma emerged, she straightened and fluffed the sheet to give the best impression of snow. She rolled on her back to find Colin standing above her with his hand stretched out.

No sooner did she take it, she found herself next to his chest. His scent was more than she could handle and dared not look at him. "Thank you." With a twist, her hand released and she sat on the couch where he joined her.

Colin spread his arms across the top edge of the couch. "We did a good job."

She leaned against his side. "We did, Mr. Brockman. We did."

"Maybe we should have waited for the team to get here. This might've been an excellent exercise for working together."

Emma snapped back without thinking. "No. This was ours." She peeked at Colin, who cocked a brow. She lifted her drink to her mouth. Before taking a sip, she muttered, "Maybe." She needed to deflect. "What type of exercises did you plan for your team?"

Colin described the research he'd found on various team-building websites, all designed to encourage employees to trust one another. She tried to act interested by nodding but found the subject boring. The hot toddy, along with her skating and the long day, caught up with her. Right in the middle of his dissertation, she rested her head against his chest and fell asleep.

In the twilight, she floated until her head fell back against something soft. Her body swayed as her feet were lifted to remove her shoes. Her lids fluttered open to find Colin standing over her pulling a comforter to her shoulders.

"You fell asleep. I carried you to your bed."

She grasped his wrist and stared into his intoxicating orbs. If he rejected her next request, she'd be embarrassed and could never face him again. The words hovered on the tip of her tongue, then flowed off. "Don't leave."

A flutter stirred deep within. She waited.

"Are you sure?"

"Yes."

Colin sat on the edge of the bed, tilted his head, and bent over to kiss her.

CHAPTER 22

THE PHONE ON the nightstand near Emma's head chirped. She squinted at the clock— 9:00 a.m. Colin snuggled alongside. The weight of his arm across her waist held her in place.

She lifted Colin's arm, grabbed the phone as she slid out of bed, and padded to the bathroom. She closed the door behind her. "Hello, Charlie. What's up?"

"I thought you should know that I have a van full of people and I'm on my way to the lodge."

His words swirled in the air. She took a few seconds to grasp their meaning and replied, "How far away are you?"

"Fifteen, twenty minutes."

Oh. No.

She opened the door and scrutinized the bed that held a naked, sleeping man.

The team couldn't find out what happened last night—what she and Colin did. If Margaret caught on, their jobs would be history. "Charlie, thanks for calling. I'll see you soon."

Emma slipped into her robe and charged to the bed. "Colin." She shook his shoulders. "Get up."

His muscular arms reached for her and pulled her across him. "Kinda a harsh way to wake a guy up." He tried to kiss her.

She blocked him by planting her palms flat on his chest. "Charlie just called.

He has your team in the van and they're almost here."

Colin's eyes popped wide open, he released her and propped himself on his elbows. "I never called Margaret to tell them to come. Why are they here?"

Knowing Margaret, she'd taken things into her own hands trying to set them up. Emma jumped off the bed. "I don't know, but I'm sure Margaret has a plan." From the first day they met in Human Resources, at Emma's job interview, Margaret seemed to have something against her.

"Where's my clothes?"

"Everywhere." Emma scurried around and gathered up Colin's clothes. She shoved the pile into his arms as he stood by the bed. "Here."

He let the bundle fall to the floor and this time his arms reached their mark. He held her close and she melted. His lips pressed to her cheek. "I'll miss you."

Her heart broke. All she wanted was to roll back into bed with him at her side and never leave. "We can't."

"I know." His mouth covered hers and a shiver raced through every inch of her body.

About to encircle, his neck he grabbed her wrist. "We can't."

She sighed. "I know."

He bent down to pick up the clothes. "I'll wait in my room. After they arrive I'll come downstairs to greet them."

As he walked away, she longed for more of the man she was falling in love with.

"When you hear them come in, that'd be a good time."

He turned and blew her a kiss. "Later."

She watched as he ascended the stairs and could only wish their future held a 'later.' In her soul, she realized their passion was destined to be a one-night stand and her heartbreak.

After she dressed, she calmed her raging nerves by pacing the wooden planks in the kitchen and gnawed at her fingernails. She glared at the clock. Charlie had said fifteen or twenty minutes, but it's been over thirty. "What's taking so long?"

"Emma, aren't they here yet?" Colin stood at the rail of the second story that overlooked the great room.

The recognizable thump of a car door came from the driveway. She raced to the window to see the team being helped out of the van by Charlie. "Colin." She darted back to find him waiting by the rail. "They're here." She made a waving motion for him to hide. "Remember, don't come out right away."

He raised a hand as he retreated to his bedroom.

Emma inhaled, then exhaled, attempting to compose herself. If she kept it together, she and Colin's secret need never be made public.

"Hi." Emma opened the back door to greet Colin's management team. "This is a surprise. We weren't expecting you."

Margaret's nose pointed in the air as if she sniffed a rancid odor.

"Colin is upstairs in his room. He didn't tell me he called you. We didn't even know the road was clear." A huge mistake on their part, one of them should've checked last night, but the tree decorating, hot toddies, and their toss in the hay interfered.

Margaret spun around, nose higher in the air. "Colin? Don't you mean Mr. Brockman and when did he arrive?"

Emma pretended not to hear the Witch's question. She gave Emma the once over, which always shook Emma's self-confidence. Margaret took every opportunity to bully her.

"He didn't call me. I checked, and the report stated they cleared the road last night. So, I contacted everyone, and we took a flight out early this morning." Margaret checked out the kitchen, then flung one end of her scarf over her shoulder. "After you show us to our rooms, you can make our coffee and breakfast."

Again came the once-over. Why on earth did she think I'd cook her breakfast or that I even knew how to cook? Emma's skin crawled. Maybe she should hit the kitchen and give Margaret food poisoning which might be a very likely outcome. She wanted to punch Margaret right in her pointed nose.

"What a beautiful tree." Jan stood by the counter with her hands clasped in front of her.

"Col..." Emma glanced at Margaret. "Mr. Brockman and I decorated it last night. We thought it'd add something to the retreat."

"Everything looks handmade."

Emma gave a quick rundown on their creativity.

"Red paint." Jan pointed toward the back door. "That's what's in the snow. I wasn't sure what it was and got freaked."

Emma laughed. "No pinecones were harmed in the process."

Margaret cleared her throat. "Our rooms."

Emma's jaw muscles tightened but she forced a sliver of a smile. "If you'll follow me, all your rooms are upstairs."

Almost at the top, Colin appeared, tucking his shirt into his jeans. "Hi, everyone. This is a surprise."

Margaret pushed Emma into the wall to make her way up the stairs to stand next to Colin.

Emma tried to figure out Margaret's strategy. That woman always had ulterior motives.

"I didn't hear from you, so I took it upon myself to get us up here a day early when I discovered the road had been cleared." Margaret shrugged her shoulders. "That way we could get finished earlier and return home to our families for our Christmas preparations."

Emma seriously doubted Margaret had any family at home and watched her bat her eyelashes at Colin.

Colin rubbed his hands together. "Great. I'm glad you're all here. Is anyone hungry?"

The group responded with "Yes."

"Emma, please show everyone to their rooms. And once you're settled in, we'll all meet in the kitchen," he announced as he walked right passed her as if she didn't matter.

In that instant, Emma became the dutiful assistant in front of the team. "Everyone. This way, please."

Margaret's room assignment came last. Emma stopped and opened the door. "I'm sure you'll find everything you need."

"Which room is Mr. Brockman's?"

Strange question to ask, but Emma pointed to the door across the hall.

Margaret gave the door a once over—that nose working the air. "And your room?"

"Downstairs. Why?"

"No reason." Margaret stepped inside and stared at her without blinking. A smirk preceded Margaret slamming the door in her face. A fist struck Emma right in the sternum. She swallowed hard. Not expecting a closed door this soon.

Emma detested that woman and spun on her heels as she marched to the kitchen.

Colin stood alone at the counter cutting vegetables. As soon as she was within reach, he grabbed her by the waist and kissed the tip of her nose. "And how are you doing?"

Emma pushed to put distance between them, but Colin held tight. "Someone might catch us. A few seconds ago, you'd treated me like a doorstop. Now you want to be all friendly again?"

"Doorstop? What else was I supposed to do? Kiss you." He peeked at the upstairs rail. "They're busy settling in." He bent over until his lips captured hers.

His touch sent her body into overdrive. She wanted more. What was she doing? She couldn't risk being caught kissing him. "Colin." She broke free of his arms. "I can't take the chance. We need to stay away from each other."

He inhaled. "Okay. I'm sorry. You're right"

"Thanks for understanding." She picked up the coffee carafe and walked to the sink. She glanced over her shoulder to study Colin's back. "I'll get the coffee started."

His quick agreement sent her little red flags flying. A sinking sensation settled in her gut. She shut her eyes for a moment. Had he been playing with her to get her in bed? The boundary lines between her ex's and Colin's behavior started to blur.

With the team assembled at the breakfast table, Colin ran down the different exercises he planned for the group.

Emma watched Margaret hang on to his every word. She giggled at his subtle jokes and made cute comments. Her behavior was out of character.

She tried to figure out what Margaret was up to. She knew that woman was plotting something.

"All right, our experience starts right now, with kitchen clean-up." Colin placed his palms on the table and stood. Everyone picked up their plates and headed toward the kitchen.

Emma walked over to Colin and stood next to him, their backs to the team. "What would you like me to do?"

He leaned in close. "I can't tell you. You asked me to keep my distance."

She stiffened and gave him a stern glare.

"You okay?"

"I'm fine." She lied. Between her mixed emotions over Colin and Margaret's blatant show of disdain, how could she be fine?

"Go do anything you'd like. Go skating and come back for lunch. You don't need to be here for the rest of this stuff."

"Good." She observed Margaret standing at the counter watching them. While the rest of the team members put food away and loaded the dishwasher, Margaret shoved her plate at Jeff and said, "Be a dear and take care of this for me."

What didn't that woman understand about team building? "Watch Margaret. She not doing her part."

"I'm already on it."

Emma skated for two hours and hid in her room afterward. Right before noon, she heard a gentle tap on the door.

"Hi, Emma. Mr. Brockman, I mean Colin." Jan stood in the hallway and waved her hand. "He asked us to call him Colin. I still need to get used to that. Anyway, he asked me to get you. We're ready to make lunch."

Emma always liked Jan. She was polite and respected personal boundaries, the exact opposite of Margaret. Who interjected herself into any situation. "Thank you. I'll be right out."

In the kitchen, everyone hustled about, doing their part to put their meal together. Except for Margaret. She commanded Colin's attention in the great room. He had his back to Emma with his arms folded, listening to Margaret who sat on the arm of the loveseat. She had Emma in her sight, then she threw her head back and laughed while placing her hand on Colin's arm.

Emma didn't know what was so funny or why Margaret played up to Colin. But Margaret's actions grated at her nerves. Margaret glanced at Emma with a smirk as she reached for Colin's hand.

Blood rushed up the back of Emma's neck and she balled her fist because Colin didn't bulk at any of Margaret's attempts at physical contact. In that instant, she realized her tense posture might give away her feelings for Colin. She lowered her head and joined the group in the kitchen. "What can I do to help?"

With their lunch finished, the group cleared the table and started planning dinner. Cooking meals together came under Colin's plan for team building. Emma gave him credit because that was a good idea.

Everyone moved about the kitchen investigating the refrigerator and the pantry to propose ideas, while Jan wrote the choices on a yellow pad. It didn't take long to create a menu for a few days.

Margaret stood next to Colin at the counter during this entire process. From her strategic location, she'd make an occasional comment to appear as though she'd participated.

The group moved to the great room for the afternoon session and left Emma standing in the kitchen, alone. As she'd predicted, the second she opened the back door to greet the team, she'd been demoted back to the position of the hired help, whose job was to observe from the outside in. A different concept she and Colin share from the confines of their offices.

CHAPTER 23

MARGARET CLUNG TO Colin's arm. He hated how she touched him and wouldn't let go. For the sake of the retreat's success, he'd put up with her advances and then politely step out of reach.

He watched Emma slip out of the kitchen and disappear around the corner. This morning, whenever he had any opportunity to talk to her, Margaret managed to monopolize the situation.

He'd wanted to spend one last day with Emma before their worlds collided back into the reality of their work positions. When she'd asked him to stay away, he understood. Margaret could make their lives miserable if she found out they broke the cardinal fraternization rule. He figured he'd be fine if the company let him go, but Emma might not be as fortunate.

"Colin, what do you have planned for this afternoon?" Margaret tightened her grip.

He reached to peel her hand from his arm. "Why don't you sit here and I'll announce that to everyone." He scanned the group and began to explain his plan for the afternoon's activities.

Laughter emerged at the end of the session to the point of tears from some members. Colin stood taller, confident his strategy was working. Several of the directors appeared more comfortable addressing him by his first name, while others invited him to join in their conversations. Whatever they experienced back at the office, their present surroundings helped to break that down.

That is, except for Margaret. She acted at participating but never did. That was fuel for his fire.

He glanced at his watch, 4:00 p.m. “Let’s call it a day. How about we meet in the kitchen around six? Take some time for a walk or use the pool table downstairs. There’s also a hot tub. Enjoy some of the amenities the lodge has to offer.”

The group dispersed in different directions, except for Margaret. “Colin.” She stepped forward and with a snake-like motion, she slinked close to his side. “Would you like to take a walk with me?”

Colin smiled, staying in diplomatic form. All he wanted to do was get away from her and find Emma, but he realized he’d have to be very discrete. “Thank you, but I think I’ll go check emails in my room and call my mother. However, could we talk?”

“What is it?”

“I’m going to be blunt here. You need to be more of an active player in the sessions.”

The hand of shock covered her chest. “What do you mean? I’m taking part.”

“Are you? Asking one of the other directors to clear your dishes or sitting on a stool while everyone helps in the kitchen is not participating. Should I continue?”

She didn’t say a word. Her eyes narrowed.

“In the meeting I held before the retreat, I explained how this activity was directly related to your upcoming performance review. Do you understand?” He needed to make sure she understood what was expected so she couldn’t play dump. The notes from the meeting served as further proof. He crossed his t’s and dotted his i’s.

She huffed. “Yes.”

He hoped she’d leave. That didn’t happen. Colin excused himself, walked up the stairs, and before he closed the door, he had his phone in hand.

“Yes sir.”

“Hey, Em.” Just her voice lifted his spirits.

"Can I help you? Do you need something?"

He paced. "No. I just wanted to see if you're okay."

"I'm fine, and thank you for asking."

Emma's brief responses made him leery to push a conversation about them spending the night together. "We're meeting in the kitchen to start dinner around six."

"Okay. Is there anything else?"

"No."

"Six it is." She clicked off.

Colin flopped across the bed, phone in hand. Did he read her signals the wrong way? They'd slept together, she'd acted as if she enjoyed herself, and cared about him.

At dinner prep, Emma stayed clear of him. She walked to the other side of the counter when he came close. She answered every question the group members asked. In front of him, she reverted to work mode minus their office-mate banter. He'd have no chance to talk to her until they were alone. If he even had the opportunity to get her alone.

Emma's skin crawled. A golf ball lodged in her throat, but she had to keep up a good front. Her dream of Emma's Attic was within reach and nothing, not even her stupid decision to sleep with Colin, would get in her way. Despite her internal turmoil, she maintained a congenial attitude and vowed to herself she'd survive dinner.

Margaret sat next to Colin, of course. Emma chuckled to herself. Yep, Margaret was determined.

What if she was interested in him romantically? Or was she just playing a game to trap him and get him to slip up?

They did have similar management positions in different departments, and if they disclosed their relationship, they'd be free to do whatever. Emma watched Colin laugh at Margaret's lame jokes.

Was he playing along or was he interested?

Would a relationship with Margaret be so bad? He deserved to be with someone. If he did play Emma only to jump her bones, maybe Margaret was what he needed. Another snake.

She pondered that idea for two seconds. *Nah.* Emma would die if they became a couple. No doubt about it—she'd go belly up because Emma wouldn't wish a snake-like Margaret on anyone. Besides, Colin was too nice even if his motives weren't honorable.

After they cleaned the kitchen, the group trudged downstairs to watch a movie. Emma attempted to sneak back to her room, but Colin insisted she join the group. Being around Colin, without being with him, caused her stomach to twist so much that she had trouble swallowing her dinner.

Work mode. You're in work mode, became her mantra, and part of that consisted of minimal interactions with the group. She'd join them for the movie but sit in the back. Once the lights dimmed she'd slip out.

Twenty minutes into an action movie, Emma snuck out of the media room. After a quick stop at the bar for some bourbon, she had everything necessary for a night of serious romance novel reading.

She entered her dark bedroom and stood in the stillness. Her shoulders slackened with heavy arms. A single tear slid down her cheek. She shook her head, wiped her face, and headed for the bathroom. A hot bath and four fingers in the glass might relax her body, but would they boost her depressed mood?

At 2:30 a.m. she lay awake in the dark with her finished romance novel opened across her chest. She flung off the covers, stepped into her slippers, and headed downstairs for the bar.

A single light in the kitchen lit the way. About to flick on the light in the game room, she noticed a figure sitting on the couch facing the windows. It was Colin. "Why are you sitting in the dark?"

He jumped and turned. "Geez, you surprised me. Come sit down." He padded the seat next to him. "Bring a glass. I have refreshments." He raised a bottle. "And don't turn on the lights. The view of the mountains in the moonlight is magnificent."

She retrieved a fresh glass off a shelf, filled it with ice, and joined him. She panned the floor-to-ceiling windows. He was right. The view was stunning.

A full moon hung in the sky just above the distant mountain range. Moonbeams hit the untouched snow and glistened in the breeze as though thousands of stars had settled on the white mantle. She stood mesmerized for a few seconds before her gaze settled on Colin's silhouette. "You couldn't sleep either."

"Nope." He nudged the bottle toward her.

He poured, and she settled back against the cushion. "You know I'm not trying to ignore you."

"Uh-huh," she muttered before sipping the bourbon.

"What?"

She blinked, inhaled, then exhaled. "Colin, I'm so close. I can't let anything get in the way."

"Close to what?"

"My plans." She shook her head and started talking. For at least fifteen minutes, Emma divulged her plans for Emma's Attic. "I've been planning this since before my divorce."

He shifted his position to face her. "All the time we spent together at those sales and you never told me? Are you afraid the loss of your job might put an end to your plans?"

She sniffled, close to tears.

Colin wrapped an arm around her shoulder and pulled her close. She nestled her head on his chest. Even if he did use her for sex, she needed his closeness and warmth right then.

She couldn't deny, in his arms, she felt secure. The steady thump of his heart created a sense of peace until a creak on the stairs behind them caused both to move apart and sit up straight. They studied the area toward the back of the room. "Do you see anyone?"

Colin stood. "No." He held out his hand for her. "Must be a house noise." She saw his line of sight never veered from the stairs. "Let's get you back to your room."

Emma led the way. Near her room, Colin stroked her upper arm before he spun her to face him. He cupped her cheeks and bent to kiss her. She didn't resist and stretched on her tippy toes to prolong their brief contact. The embrace and his warm lips melted her inside.

As he pulled away, she saw movement behind them. "Someone's at the end of the hall."

He pivoted. Where the hallway opened to the great room, he flipped on the lights and began to search. He disappeared around the corner.

She folded her arms and bit her lip. She suspected the only person sneaky enough to snoop, the one person who had the power to fire them if she caught them together. Margaret.

CHAPTER 24

THE NEXT MORNING Margaret waited at the base of the stairs for Colin to descend. She uncoiled and slithered close. "We need to talk."

His nerves prickled. He observed her nose-in-the-air superior-profile, which convinced him she had slithered around in the dark last night. "Sure. We can talk in the study. I'll meet you there after I get my coffee. Would you like a cup?"

That nose popped up. "No. I'm fine."

He stood at the counter and stirred his coffee longer than necessary. The simple action provided time to prepare for battle.

Margaret proved to be a challenge. Her lack of participation in group activities was feeble. That showed she failed as a team player, and he could use that on her evaluation, but that wasn't enough to dismiss her.

The woman thrived on drama. Daily, she'd have a crisis to solve. On more than one occasion, she'd drag him into the issue of her own making, convinced his intervention was necessary. His patience was at a breaking point, but he needed solid evidence. Until then, he'd play along.

If Margaret was the one sneaking around last night, his and Emma's futures with the Pendleton Group could be the ones in jeopardy. If she felt caged, she'd retaliate against them and their embrace gave her the perfect reason to attack them. *How could I let this happen*?

He downed a healthy swig of his brew and headed for the study.

"What can I help you with?"

She straightened, moved to the edge of the wing-backed chair positioned in front of the desk, and folded her hands over her knee. "I came upon some rather disturbing information last night."

Colin walked to the other side of the desk and sat, taking his management posture. She'd just confirmed she'd crept on the lower-level stairs. He waited for her to drop the bomb. "Okay. What is this information?"

"This is uncomfortable to talk about. I'm not sure how I should express my concern over the problem."

He leaned back in the chair. Yeah, her concern was a joke. He'd have to play her game for her to provide the information on her own time, although he was positive that he already knew. "Why not just tell me what's on your mind?"

She squirmed when she shifted positions. Her nose shot higher into the air. "I thought since you are my immediate supervisor, I'd do you the courtesy of coming to you first before I took the information to Mr. Pendleton."

"I appreciate that. Please go on." Yep. She's the sneaky one. Her righteous act grated at him. He'd been here, done that with her many times in his office during one of her emergencies. However, this was different. He'd never been the one in her sights, waiting for her to strike.

"Last night."

Colin braced for the bomb.

She pursed her lips before she opened her mouth and ran her tongue over her upper lip. Next, she smoothed her pant leg and moved her squinted glare around the room. Colin patiently watched all the dramatic gesturing.

"Margaret." He waved a hand for her to talk.

She snapped her head back in his direction. "I know you and Emma have gotten close. Too close."

And there it was, the tsunami wave that would flood Emma and his worlds. "And you know this how?"

"I witnessed you."

"When?" If he could get her to admit she spied on them, she'd have to withdraw.

"I couldn't sleep and thought a glass of warm milk might help. I heard voices from downstairs and decided to investigate."

Of course, she'd nose around. Colin listened.

"Imagine my surprise to see two people sitting on the couch, in the dark, in what I'd call an inappropriate embrace." She sat erect as if a stick was stuck up her rear. "Do you have anything to say?"

They were sunk. She had a good reason to come downstairs and her story might hold up. He wanted to find out if she'd admit to seeing them at Emma's door. "Is there anything else?"

"Yes. I saw you kiss her."

He leaned forward and folded his hands on the desk. "Did you continue to spy on us?"

She snapped back, "I wouldn't call it that."

"Then what would you call it?" The hairs on the back of his neck rose.

"I'd call it sexual harassment on your part. The way you grabbed her arm and forced her to kiss you."

'Dumbfounded' didn't describe the sick sensation that washed over him. He maintained his composure even though his blood hit the boiling point. He couldn't deny he kissed Emma, but he certainly didn't take her by force. "And if I say you're lying."

"I'll take this to the top." Her nose jetted upward.

"Margaret, what do you want?"

Emma tilted her head. The voices from the study generated a red flag warning. Colin had closed the doors before the retreat and posted a sign asking the team to stay out. She walked toward the voices, prepared to ask whoever invaded the space to leave. At the base of the stairs, she stopped to listen. The voices came from Colin and Margaret.

With slow deliberate steps, she edged toward the French doors.

Margaret spoke, "I want her gone."

"Okay, so you fire her. What about me?"

"You're too important to the company. You'll be safe." Margaret's voice was slow and methodical.

Emma's hand flew to her mouth. Colin confirmed her fear. What a fool she was. She'd let another man use and betray her, then throw her away like yesterday's trash.

Their deceitful words burned into Emma's brain. That's all she had to hear. Her hands started to twitch. She spun around and ran back to her room.

Her hands shook so much that she had trouble opening the closet door. She threw the suitcase on the bed, and it bounced a few times before stopping close to the edge. She cleaned off the bathroom counter and stuffed everything with her clothes in the bag.

If she worked fast enough, she might get out of the house before anyone discovered she'd left.

The chatter from the kitchen told Emma the team had assembled for breakfast prep. Her plans for an uneventful escape diminished because she'd have to pass them on her way to the garage.

If she waited any longer, she'd risk having to deal with her two-faced boss. The "get the girl in bed, then sell her out to save yourself" jerk.

Boy, he had her fooled, playing Mr. Nice Guy for the past nine months.

At the end of the hall, she took a second to compose herself. Their tree stood tall and graceful decorated in white snowflakes, a symbol of her poor judgment. One would think she'd learned her lesson after her ex.

She grabbed the handle of her bag and prepared to enter the kitchen. The thump under her ribcage increased with each step toward her destination. The beat continued until the pulse filled her ears.

"Emma, why the suitcase?" Jan spoke up and that focused everyone's attention toward her.

"I'm scheduled to leave today. I was only asked to stay until the retreat was running on track." She never stopped advancing toward the back door. "Everyone enjoy yourselves and I'll see you back at the office." *Yeah, when I do my walk of shame as security escorts me out of the building.*

Then second her bag hit the snow covered path she picked up the pace for the garage. With a few taps on the pad, the door lifted. She wasted no time and threw her bag in the back seat of the rental car.

"Emma!"

"Oh, crap." Colin ran down the path toward the garage. With his long legs, he'd be next to the car in seconds. She slammed the back door and dropped the car fob. "No. No. No."

She scooped it up, flung open the driver's door, and jumped in. About to press the lock button, Colin opened the door.

"Where are you going?"

"Home."

"Why?"

Both her gloved hands whacked the steering wheel. She tightened her jaw and stared straight ahead. "Leave me alone and go away."

"Emma, it's cold. Come back inside so you can tell me what's going on." He rubbed his upper arms and produced a frosty mist around his nose.

How like Colin to be concerned about his comfort. Seconds passed before she pivoted her head in his direction. "Leave. Me. Alone." She squinted with a death stare and if he didn't let her go, she'd slam the door on his fingers.

His face slackened, his hand fell, and he took a step back.

Good, he listened. She took no time slamming and locking the door. She started the car, hit the gas, and drove down the winding drive.

Tears streamed down her cheek. "Not again. Not. Again."

Why didn't she recognize the signs? She'd enjoyed being around him for months and she'd convinced herself he wasn't like her ex. Then he was cornered, and his true colors came out. The rough texture of her glove scraped across her cheek. Better she found out now, but what difference did that make? She'd be the one to suffer all the consequences. Margaret made it very clear he was too important, leaving Emma to be the scapegoat. She'd lose her job and have to place her dream of opening Emma's Attic on hold indefinitely.

At least she'd dodged the Colin love bullet.

CHAPTER 25

THE ELEVATOR DOOR opened to the seventeenth floor of the Pendleton office.

A Christmas tree decked in gold and white stood next to the receptionist's desk. Christmas music filled the halls as Emma straightened her shoulders and gave the young man behind the desk a nod as she passed. The difference between today and the last time she'd strolled into work, a week ago, was her knowledge this was her last day.

She'd arrived home from that dreaded retreat two days ago. Since the team was still at the lodge and no one expected her back in the office, she decided to recoup an extra day. That gave her today, one last day to be the executive assistant of Colin Brockman until she'd be called to Margaret's domain to be fired.

Emma kept her head high and greeted her coworkers. She passed Jan's office and took a double take. *Why was Jan at her computer*? The retreat was supposed to end on the twentieth and everyone was due back on the twenty-first. Today was the twentieth, so why was Jan back a day early?

There was only one way to find out, she'd ask. "Good morning, Jan."

Jan's expression turned from content to surprise. Her hand covered her throat. "Emma. You frightened me."

"I'm sorry. What are you doing here?"

Jan walked from behind her desk and stood next to Emma. "After you left, Mr. Brockman held the morning session and then announced we'd be leaving that afternoon. The van arrived, we left for the airport, and he drove off in his car."

Emma scrutinized the hall in the direction of Colin's office. "Did he say why?"

Jan shook her head and shrugged her shoulders.

"Thanks. I hope you enjoyed the retreat." Emma headed down the hall and stepped inside the outer office. Colin's door was closed. She turned the knob. It didn't open. Then she held her ear close to the door. No sound came from his inner sanctum. She figured he might be running late but hoped he and Margaret would finish her off ASAP.

She tucked her bag in a drawer and went to fix their coffee, as she had done since his second week on the job. That was their routine.

She was still his executive assistant until the ax fell. As she carried their cups to their office, a heaviness came over her, this was the last time she'd fix his coffee. Despite his betrayal, they'd had good times, but that all ended at the lodge.

She'd have to find another job and eat into her shop fund to support herself while she came up with a new business plan.

Emma knocked on his door. No answer. She turned the knob. It remained locked. She grabbed the key and walked in to investigate.

On his desk, she placed the cup along with a few Christmas cookies from the breakroom, and the stack of mail in anticipation he'd be in soon.

She took a second to scan the office. Despite how she'd be leaving, she'd miss his morning greeting and how his inviting smile had made her day. She loved how Colin made her job more interesting just by being himself.

She couldn't deny it, even though he'd broken her heart into a million little pieces, she'd miss him. But like her other heartbreak, she'd survive and come out stronger on the other side. At least that's what her therapist taught her.

By mid-morning, Emma's nerves were frayed. There'd been no sign of Margaret or Colin. What was taking so long? She figured she'd be called into H.R. and fired as soon as the clock struck nine. Afterward, she'd collect her belongings, do the walk of shame to the elevator, and out she'd go. But there was nothing. Why?

After thirty minutes of mulling over her inevitable demise, she walked into

Colin's office to remove the cold cup of coffee. She studied the cookies before tossing them in the trash. "Some Christmas?" Just like all the others in her childhood. She'd be alone and broke.

"He's gone."

Emma spun around to find Margaret propped against the doorjamb, arms crossed. Nose in the air. She straightened and walked, taking her time, toward Emma. "I'm waiting on instructions from Colin as to what to do about you."

Emma almost dropped the cup of coffee, her words caught in her throat.

Margaret continued her approach until she circled behind Emma. "You know it's all your fault." Her voice was low.

"What are you talking about?"

"I know you slept with him."

Emma's nostrils flared. Margaret's razor tone put her on edge, but she had to keep her cool. She'd need a reference to find another job. Shoulders back, she faced the Witch.

"Margaret, are you here to fire me?"

That nose shot into the air. "No, I wanted to, but he wouldn't let me."

Emma tilted her head. "What are you talking about?"

Margaret slanted her lids and moved closer to Emma's face. "Mr. Brockman told me to wait until he came back. Although I don't see why. You're not worth keeping around."

She circled to Emma's side and leaned in close. "As long as you're still an employee with this company, I promise I'll make your remaining days here as miserable as I can."

Emma's emotions bounced from disbelief to disgust. But, after all her therapy sessions, she learned she had zero reason to be subjected to Margaret or Colin's cruelty. He wouldn't let Margaret fire her. She wasn't their plaything to toss back and forth.

She clenched her fist, nails biting into her palm and wanting to drench Margaret with the cold coffee. Seeing her surprised face would make Emma's day, but that action served no constructive purpose.

She looked Margaret straight in the eye. "I'll save you the trouble. I quit. I'll gather my things and be out of here before lunch." She walked to the door. "Merry Christmas. You're getting what you wanted—early."

After Colin dismissed the team, he drove to Calgary, flew back to Houston, and drove straight to Sugar Land. He tried to text and call Emma, but she dismissed his attempts.

Rob and Colin sat in the spacious great room of the Pendleton mansion in Sugar Land, Texas, a suburb of Houston.

"I'm not sure I understand." Rob raised his eyebrows. "You want a demotion, so Emma won't lose her job."

Colin nodded. "That's right."

"What happened at the lodge?"

Colin adjusted his position and provided all the details that led to his hasty departure to Houston. "She's so close to opening her shop, and without any income, that might not happen."

Rob sank into the chair. "Son, you know I'll do whatever you want, but I have one question. Have you told her you love her?"

Colin pulled back. His stomach knotted.

"You do love her?" Rob sported that grin he always had when he knew he was right about something.

Colin's emotions whirled whenever Em came into his thoughts. In fact, she never left and was there just walking around like an extra voice in his head.

"Of course, I do." Colin leaned forward and braced his hands on his knees. "She won't talk to me. I've tried texting and calling, but all I get is crickets."

"That could be a problem." Rob stood. "Until you clear things up with her, you and she won't find peace."

Sandra, Rob's wife made a grand entrance in a way only the matriarch of a family can. "Colin, my darling, how are you."

"Very well, thanks, Mom number two." Colin shot to his feet. He adored the petite woman who took him under her wing when he moved to Texas.

She placed her hand on his arm. "That will never get old. You know I love you like a son and Robert has some competition."

That put a smile on his face and satisfied him, that he held a place in his best friend's mother's heart.

"By the way, how is your mother?"

"Alive and well in sunny California. She came to visit this summer."

Sandra's brow rose. Her interior design persona emerged. "I suspect rented furniture filled the place."

Colin roared a hardy laugh. "Not this time. I have an apartment filled with *my* furniture."

"What?"

"Em likes to shop yard and garage sales and helped me fix up the place."

She patted his arm. "Tell your mother I said hello. Who's Em?"

Rob snapped, "Boy's got girl trouble."

Sandra's expression brightened. "You don't say. It's about time."

"He's in love but she won't talk to him," Rob tossed in.

Colin swung around to give Rob a scowling glare. "You're not helping."

Sandra giggled under her breath. "Colin, he'll never change."

Then she focused on Rob. "Darling, will you be much longer? Robert texted. He and Belinda are on their way. You need to get some steaks on and Colin, I want all the juicy details at dinner."

"Yes, Ma'am."

A tight grin spread across her face as she left.

Colin's phone pinged. *Problem solved. Emma quit!*

A pain stabbed Colin's gut.

"Something wrong?" Rob faced Colin, his hands in his pockets.

"It's from Margaret. Em quit." Colin showed him the message.

"Text Margaret to find out what happened?"

Colin tapped in the text and they waited.

A few seconds later, Margaret responded, *I went to your office and she became angry when I told her you wanted to wait to fire her. Her face flared red, told me she quit, packed her things, and left.*

Colin flopped against the couch's back. “Rob, Margaret is trouble. She threatened to file a sexual harassment complaint against me, claiming I forced Emma to kiss me.” He tapped his fingers on the couch arm. “Something like that could ruin me and cause trouble for you.”

“Well, did you force her?”

“Hell no. You should know better.”

Rob smiled and appeared unconcerned.

Colin knitted his brow. “What do you know that I don’t?”

“Son, this isn’t my first rodeo with a bad manager. Especially employees I inherit when I buy a company. Some are loyal and others are out for revenge. I don’t know which one drives Margaret. We talked about how she isn’t a good fit for that office. She’s what I call toxic.”

“But I don’t have enough to dismiss her. She’s smart and sneaky.”

“I told you so.” Rob joined Colin on the couch and leaned in closer. “Now, fill me in on her shenanigans.”

For the next half-hour, Colin dove right into what he’d documented and discussed with Margaret about her management practices.

“Are there any employees, ex or current, who will testify to what you told me is true?”

Colin rubbed his jaw. “I think a current employee Georgia Ballenger. She’s Emma’s friend and Margaret’s assistant. Maybe the two Margaret fired a few months back.”

“We need to get solid information.” He slapped his knee. “As far as Emma goes. Can’t help you there.” He hesitated a few seconds before he raised a finger to make his point. “Or maybe I can. You told me she’s a good people manager and understands company policy.”

“Yeah. She is and she does.”

He made a waving motion with his hands before he clasped them. “Now, this is just a thought. Do you think she’d become my new H.R. Director?”

Colin stopped to mull over the idea. “I don’t know. That might interfere with her opening her shop.” He shook his head. “I just don’t know.”

Rob sighed. “Understood. From what you told me, I’m sure Emma is boiling mad and she'll need time to calm down. Besides, we only got the short version of the conversation between Margaret and Emma/ And we can both agree the source is not reliable." He winked. "Here's the plan."

Colin listened.

As Rob finished, he focused on Colin. "We clear?"

"Crystal." Colin became filled with a microcosm of hope.

CHAPTER 26

ON DECEMBER TWENTY-FIRST, Emma signed the lease for the future home of Emma's Attic. She clutched the papers in her hands. "Georgia, I can't believe I did this." She waved the document over her head. "Merry Christmas to me" She reached for Georgia's hand. "Thank you for coming with me."

Emma stopped. Georgia wasn't sharing her enthusiasm. "What's wrong?"

"I'm concerned about you. Ever since grade school, you've been a planner. Signing the lease seems like you didn't give this much thought."

Emma scoffed, clutched the lease, and slammed her hand to her side. "I can't believe you're saying this. You're the one who always told me I was afraid. You told me I didn't want to leave Colin." She threw her hands up in the air. "Well, he's not here. And you know why? He's saving his skin by throwing me to the wolves."

"Emma, don't be angry with me. You know I'm here for you and always will be."

Tears formed and rolled down Emma's cheeks. "I'll have you know, I did give signing this a lot of thought. Dollar signs are twirling in my head. I'm dreaming about the numbers and I think I'll have enough money for one year. If I can't make the shop work when this lease is up, I'll close it and walk away."

Georgia squeezed her hand. "What can I do to help?"

"Be my friend." Emma wiped her face and then dangled the keys from a finger. “Should we go and see what my signature on the dotted line gets me?”

The pair walked into an open space covered in dust. Piles of boxes full of paper, clothes, and junk covered the floor.

“Em. What was in here before?”

“I don’t know but I think the last tenants used this for overflow storage. The landlord said I could do whatever I wanted with it.” She walked around and poked at a few of the items. From one of the boxes, she pulled a lace tablecloth that was dirty but otherwise in good condition. “Georgia, I might be able to find some of the store’s inventory in these boxes.”

She opened the tablecloth to inspect it. “Look, nothing’s wrong. It just needs a wash.”

At the same time, they smiled at each other. “Em. This could save you a bunch of money.”

“No kidding.”

“Hey, I have to get back to work. Tomorrow, I can help you after I get off.”

“I’d appreciate that.” Heaven knows she’d need all the help Georgia could offer and with Georgia by her side, at least she wouldn’t second guess herself.

The sun hung in the morning sky as Emma opened the door to her new shop. She wasted no time and lined up tradespeople to transform the shop’s interior as well as starting the process of registering the business with the City of Toronto. Of course, the trades, pulling permits, and a work start date had to wait until after the holiday season.

She couldn’t wait for all the government bureaucracy and the trades. That afternoon, armed with cleaning supplies, Emma tackled the mess the previous renters had left behind. Maybe she couldn’t paint or build shelves, but she knew how to clean and couldn’t wait to search through her newfound treasure boxes.

Colin waited for Georgia in his outer office. “Georgia, thank you for coming. I’d like to introduce you to Mr. Pendleton.”

Her face went white, but she shook his hand.

"Let's go inside." The trio entered Colin's office. "Please take a seat." He directed her to the seating area while he closed the door behind them just in case Margaret decided to make an uninvited appearance. "Would you like something to drink?"

"No thank you." She maintained a straight posture but her foot tapped the floor after she sat on the couch and rested her clasped hands on her knee.

"Rob, how about you?"

"Water, please."

Colin returned and placed the drinks on the coffee table. He glanced at Georgia. Despite his attempts to put her at ease, she had to be terrified. Colin sat next to Georgia while Rob sat in a chair. "I bet you're wondering why you're here."

Her voice cracked. "I am."

Rob leaned forward and rested his arms on his knees. "It's come to my attention that there've been some improprieties in the H.R. department."

Georgia scooted to the edge of the couch. "Sir, I can assure you I have been a loyal employee and I'd never..."

Rob raised a hand for her to stop talking. "I need your help."

Georgia studied the men. She ran her palms on the front of her slacks. "What kind of help?"

"With your boss."

Georgia's mouth slacked. "I don't understand."

If Rob didn't handle the next question right and Colin misjudged Georgia's loyalty to the company and Emma, Margaret could have grounds to sue the firm.

A sliver of a smile emerged. Georgia sat back, relaxed her posture, and crossed her legs. She tilted her head. "Tell me more."

Rob shot a concerned glance at Colin. Colin got the message and jumped in to continue with an explanation. "This is a delicate matter..."

Georgia spoke, "I know more about her than I care to know. So, what can I do for you?"

Colin smiled. Georgia was in.

"We need her gone and we need hard evidence to dismiss her." Rob leaned in closer to stress his point.

Georgia panned between the two men. “May I use your computer?”

“Sure.” Colin stood.

“Pull the screen down. I’ll project everything. Make sure that door is locked.”

Colin secured the door and pushed the button which lowered the screen above the credenza.

“What’s she up to?” Rob asked.

“I have no idea.”

From Colin’s desk Georgia ordered, “Close those blinds so you can see.”

First, she pulled up pictures. Colin scrutinized the first image. He’d seen this before. It was on the flash drive Sam took back to Houston. “So, she has pictures of public places?”

Georgia huffed and walked over with a laser pointer she picked up from Colin’s deck. “This is Sally.” A red dot circled the figure. “And this is Keith.”

Colin's mind reeled.

“Now here they are, but they're holding hands.” She went to the next slide. “In this picture, they're stealing a kiss.”

“How did you get these?”

A devious smile spread across her face. She clicked the mouse button to progress to the next picture. “I stole them. Colin, you’ll like this one.”

His eyes grew wide. On the screen, he saw himself and Emma sitting at the coffee shop the day he called Margaret on her verbal misconduct. Mouth open, he popped against the back of the couch.

“This one’s even better.”

Projected on the screen was a picture of Colin and Emma standing by his car in the parking garage when he placed the throw around her shoulders. Colin moved to the edge of the couch and rubbed his hand over his mouth, floored by the image. “That’s a picture from my first day.”

“You ready for more? Here are her last two expense reports. I fill those out for her.” She used the pointer to highlight an expense. “This meal coincided with the time you and Em were at the coffee shop. She was sitting outside, at the same shop having lunch while she took a few pictures in between bites."

Georgia dropped her hands to her thighs and turned with a hip tilted out. "Now you tell me, how is spying on employees a legitimate business expense? She did the same when she took the pictures of Sally and Keith." She raised her finger. "And I have more of the same from when Mr. Tabor was here.

The two men sat studying the screen. "Georgia, why didn't you bring this to me earlier?"

"I wanted to, but Margaret watches me like a hawk, and with Sally and Keith gone, I barely had time to breathe. Then you all left for the retreat and Emma quit." She leaned in. "I became a one-woman show."

Colin looked at Rob. "Is this enough with what I already have?"

Rob's face lit up. "More than enough. She'd been stalking employees which is against our code of conduct. Falsifying expense reports speaks for itself."

A huge smile settled across every face in the locked room.

Later that night, Colin stood in a darkened doorway, out of the bite of the sharp wind, across the street from Emma's shop. He watched as Georgia and she had a heated discussion that ended in a hug. He hoped Georgia stuck to the plan she, Rob and he plotted out during the meeting in his office that afternoon.

When the women were in the back room, he walked across the street and taped a paper snowflake to the door.

Emma spent the afternoon picking up trash, sorting potential inventory, boxing, moving around the unusable items, and putting some major energy into dust removal. When Georgia arrived after work, they'd haul out the bigger pieces to the alley. To her surprise, she filled several boxes that didn't fall under the definition of junk. With a little tender loving care, the articles would serve as inventory for the shop.

She took a swig of water while she waited for Georgia and pulled out her computer to go over her finances. After she refigured the numbers, blood drained from her face.

From the estimates she'd gathered the harsh reality was she had underestimated her financial situation, and that slapped her in the face. The nightmares she had for the last few days of dollar signs and numbers haunting her were true. The current figures gave her six months or less to have an income-producing shop and even she knew that wasn't feasible. Most new businesses took one to two years to break even. Her impulse to get back at Margaret by quitting now assured her financial demise.

She closed her eyes and wanted to die. Georgia was right. She hadn't thought through the lease signing well enough. In six months she might be living under a bridge because she'd be bankrupt.

"Are you okay?"

Emma opened her eyes to find Georgia standing in front of her. "When did you get here?"

"I just walked in." She sat on a nearby box. "What's wrong?"

"I made a big mistake. I can't afford all of this." She waved for Georgia to come closer to view her spreadsheet and explained her dilemma.

"Can you apply for a government loan?"

"Yes, but those take time and lots of red tape for approval. Time I don't have." She studied the spreadsheet then lowered the lid on the laptop. "If I'd stuck to my original plan, all the stuff I needed to open would've been in place while I still had an income." She scanned the shop and settled her gaze on the door to the back. "I guess I could live in the storeroom if worse comes to worst. That's more appealing than under a bridge."

Georgia scoffed and backhanded her shoulder. "Or stay with me. But, I think I know a better way."

"How could you have a better way?"

"I do. Do you trust me?"

Emma always trusted Georgia. She was the only person in her life who stood by her even if she made questionable decisions. Georgia was Emma's emotional rock. "Explain."

Georgia hesitated. "It involves Colin."

Emma shot to her feet. "No. I will not ask him for anything." She marched across the shop to the counter and put her laptop down. "Georgia, why would you even suggest that?"

"I didn't." Georgia walked and stood next to her. She shoved a pile of newspapers to the side and coughed from the dust cloud they stirred up. "I want you to meet me at the office tomorrow."

"Why would I do that?"

She covered Emma's hand. "I'll tell you tomorrow if you come."

Emma saw the urgency on her face. Ever since they were kids, Georgia never held back from telling her anything. *So, why the secrecy*? "I don't understand."

Georgia's lips thinned and she placed her hand on Emma's arm. "I need you to trust me. Please agree to meet me at the office around one o'clock."

"Maybe." She shot her finger in Georgia's face. "But, only if I don't have to see Colin."

Georgia let out a sigh, lowered her head, and threw her hands in the air. "We'll have to meet in his office."

"Oh. No." Emma waved her hands in a frenzied motion in front of her and started to pace. Georgia had to be nuts to expect her to be anywhere near that man. Anger couldn't begin to explain the rage boiling inside. He'd be the last person on earth she'd ask for help.

"Emma, calm down."

She clasped her hands to stop the shaking. "Why? Do you know what you're asking of me?"

Georgia pulled back her shoulders and planted her hands on her hips. She widened her stance before her voice hardened. "I know exactly what I'm asking." She took two steps forward. "I'm asking you to be reasonable and to stop acting like a child."

Emma had no words. At that point, she should've thrown Georgia out of the store. "I'm not acting like a child."

"No? You're throwing a temper tantrum right now."

Georgia's words slapped her face. "How dare you! He hurt me and doesn't even care."

"What did he do?"

"I told you."

"You only told me part of the story." She held her thumb and forefinger close and squinted one eye. "The teeny-weeny part you heard before you stormed out. What else do you know? Heck, I know more about what happened than you do."

Emma stood speechless. She had drawn all her conclusions from the overheard portion of the conversation between Colin and Margaret.

"Have you answered any of Colin's calls or texts?" Georgia got in Emma's face. "Well, have you."

Emma lowered her head. Ashamed she'd been so hotheaded. "No."

"Did you know he was willing to take a demotion and move back to Houston so you wouldn't be fired?"

Emma's shoulders slackened. She lowered herself to sit on a box. "What?"

"That's why he wasn't in the office when you got back. He was in Houston trying to save your sorry ass, not his." Georgia rolled her eyes to the ceiling.

"I'm a fool."

"You took the words right out of my mouth." Georgia sat and took Emma's hand, but didn't say anything.

The pair sat in silence until Georgia spoke in a low voice, "You know I'd never do anything to hurt you. Come to the office tomorrow."

"I guess. In all fairness I should hear what he has to say."

"Good. Thank you, Emma. This means a lot to me and it will for you too."

"Why?"

"Show up tomorrow and you'll find out." She caressed Emma's hand as they sat in the quiet of the empty store for a few moments.

Emma had been the biggest fool on earth for not talking to him. All she saw was an ex-husband who belittled her until she had no self-esteem left. But she wasn't that person any longer and Colin wasn't her ex. He deserved to be heard because in the months she knew him he never did anything but show her consideration and respect.

Georgia scanned their surroundings and planted her palms on her knees.

“Okay. Let’s finish getting this stuff hauled out.”

They stood and faced each other. “Georgia, thank you.” Emma threw her arms around Georgia’s neck. “You’re a good friend and I love you.” Her eyes burned as moisture accumulated. “Let’s get going. Unlike me, you have a job, which means getting up early.”

With the last of the garbage cleared, Georgia left. Emma stood in a shop devoid of any sign of the former occupants except for a stack of neatly packed boxes of future sale items. She was determined to find a way to open even if she had to find another job and move in with Georgia.

She flipped off the lights and opened the front door to find a piece of paper taped to the glass, an advertisement or neighborhood announcement. One quick tug released the trash. About to crumble the paper she stopped to find she held a paper snowflake made out of copy paper. She checked both sides for a written message but the snowflake was blank.

Her breath hitched as she stepped to the middle of the sidewalk. She searched up and down the street which produced nothing.

“Colin,” floated past her lips and regret filled her heart.

CHAPTER 27

COLIN CHECKED HIS watch and stared at Georgia. "You did tell her one."

"I did. She promised me she'd come."

He sucked in air. She had to come. He had to talk to her. He missed her and this might be his last chance to have her as part of his life.

Nerves on edge, he stood to face the painting that hung behind his desk when he heard the faint knock. He spun and two-stepped to the inner office door. His hand encircled the knob, but he took a second to calm his jumping insides. When ready, he opened the door. "Emma."

She clutched her coat close. Her sexy, brown hair fell around her shoulders. Her soft brown eyes sparkled, and, as always, she was beautiful.

"Please come in. Let me take your coat." He hung it on one of the padded hangers in the closet reserved for his suit jackets. "Please, sit down."

They walked in silence and she took a seat in one of the chairs in front of his desk. Georgia sat in the other and she reached to squeeze Emma's hand. "Thank you."

Emma nodded in recognition.

Colin walked around his desk and sat. "Well, we might as well get started." He leaned forward, "Emma, thank you for agreeing to meet me." He maintained a business-like persona. That's all he could do since he had no idea how she'd respond to him.

She raised a brow and nodded.

"Several things have happened since you left and I'd like to fill you in."

Emma raised a hand. "Shouldn't Margaret be here for this?"

"Ah. As of this morning, she's no longer with the company."

Emma swung her head toward Georgia. "Did you know about this yesterday and didn't say anything?"

"We can't talk about that. You're not an employee." She raised a brow and nudged her head in Colin's direction. "Let him finish."

Emma understood and drifted her gaze back to Colin. "Okay. Go on."

"What would you think about coming back part-time as the Director of Human Resources?"

"That's a full-time position."

"It is unless you share the position with someone else."

"Whom would I be sharing with?"

"Me," Georgia chimed in and bounced to the edge of her chair, all smiles.

Emma knitted her brow.

"Em, it's easy. I know all the paperwork. You know the policies inside and out. For the next few months, we'd work together while you teach me about the inner workings of the company. Then when I'm ready, I take over as the full-time Director and you run your store. It's perfect. But until then you have an income."

Emma sat back against the chair and studied Colin. "Is this your idea?"

"Actually, no, it's Rob Pendleton's. He realized there needed to be a change and this is what he proposed."

"Em, think about it. We'll split the H.R. Director's salary which is more than either of us was made as assistants. We'll both get a raise. You'll be able to leave whenever you need to check on the trades, go shopping for your inventory, have money for your grand opening, and you'll be a manager." She regarded Colin. "Nothing to stand in the way of the two of you."

Colin squirmed in his seat. Georgia's comment wasn't part of the plan even though that very thought had been planted in his mind for months. He cleared his throat. "I'll step out and let you talk. When you've reached a decision, text me."

He walked out of the office and headed for the breakroom. This was a perfect solution to all of their problems. Emma had to say "yes." Georgia would be promoted to the Director of H.R. and her best friend couldn't deny Georgia her dream. Emma would have the money she needed to open her shop, and he'd get to see Emma at the office, at least for a few more months.

His phone pinged while he was halfway down the hall. "Hmm. That didn't take long." In an about-face, he headed back.

At the door to the inner office, he ran his finger around his collar, adjusted his tie, and then opened the door. "Is there a decision?"

The women swiveled to face him. He walked to his seat, trying to keep his unsettled nerves under control. "Ladies."

Emma spoke, "We agree."

He wanted to jump for joy despite the message the inappropriate display carried. "Good. I'm glad to hear this. I think this arrangement will be a satisfying solution and meet all our needs."

"I have one question," Emma said.

"Please ask."

"Now that I'm an employee I'd like to know why you fired Margaret?"

He focused on Georgia for help and she picked up on his silent plea.

"She threatened Colin with a sexual harassment complaint on your behalf and was kinda stealing some money. Then there was the stalking of employees."

Emma's pitch raised several octaves, "What?"

"Wait till you see the pictures. She said she witnessed him force you to kiss him. I also did a little digging and found out she did something similar at her last job. That company paid her to slink away. Mr. Pendleton didn't bite and now she's gone and with no extra severance."

Emma studied Colin. Her hand covered her throat. "I'm so sorry. I didn't know."

"If we're finished here, I have some termination papers to fill out and some rehire ones." Georgia stood. Emma started to stand but Georgia placed her hand on Emma's shoulder and shook her head. Emma sat back down. Georgia gave one nod toward Colin. "You two finish talking."

Alone with her, he was at a loss. He had no choice but to stay in business mode. “I’m glad you agreed to this arrangement. I think this will be a win-win for all of us.”

“Colin.” She wrung her hands and then ran them up and down her thighs. “Believe me when I say, I’m really sorry. Can you forgive me? I feel like such a fool.”

Of course, he’d forgive her. He’d wanted to take her in his arms and shower her with tiny, loving kisses all over.

Instead, he resisted. “Don’t. It’s over.”

He stood to shake her hand. “I’ll see you right after the holidays. You can go see Georgia about the paperwork.” When she took his hand, he didn’t want to let go. He wanted to hang on forever, but of course, he released it. What else could he do?

She walked to the door but he couldn’t stop himself and the words tumbled out. “Em, I miss you.”

She stopped and half turned. “Do you have any plans for Christmas Eve?”

His heart did a few flips. “None.”

“Would you like to come over for dinner? We could cook together.”

His heart stopped. “I’d love to.”

From over her shoulder, she flashed a huge smile. Her hair framed her face as a few curls draped over one eye. “On the way out, when I stop at HR, I’ll add a personal relationship disclosure to my employee file. Georgia can get your signature later today. Around seven then?”

He widened his eyes and stood speechless for a second. “Yeah. Seven.”

She twisted the knob and disappeared into the outer office. He jumped, made a few dance-like turns, and added several fist pumps.

On Christmas Eve, at seven o’clock sharp, Colin knocked on Emma’s apartment door. His nerves were in shambles.

“Right on...” She stopped and pointed. “What is that?”

Colin stood next to a three-foot fir tree decorated with a tiny white paper chain, mini glitter-tipped pinecones, a homemade foil cover star, and of course, miniature paper snowflakes.

"I thought maybe you didn't have time to decorate because you were busy with the shop and I know how much you enjoy..."

"Colin." She reached for the collar of his overcoat and pulled him to within a few centimeters of her face. "You're a wonderful man and I never want to let you go ever again, but only if you want that."

His lips hovered over hers for a second until he covered hers with his. Lip-locked they worked their way into the apartment and closed the door.

A few seconds later the door flung open. Colin picked up the miniature tree and hauled it inside.

Epilogue

THE SEASONS PAST and on Christmas Eve, Emma closed out the books for the holidays with record sales. Georgia's social media viewers helped get the shop in the sights of the surrounding communities. Several TV interviews and news articles also helped as well as the online shop. She had to hire a part-timer to handle the orders.

Then with Rob Pendleton's plan in motion, she was able to open her shop in four months and loan-free. The wonderful man even offered her a consulting position for a few extra months which allowed her to have a nice reserve in the bank.

For this upcoming week, she'd close the shop to concentrate on Colin. They had plans to relax and enjoy Christmas with a few friends and they made sure the week involved plenty of bedroom time. After Christmas, they'd fly to Calgary and drive to the lodge to spend New Year's as guests of the Pendleton family.

Her last task before rushing into the arms of the man she loved was to check inventory in the store room.

Clipboard in hand she walked back into the store to lock up. Near the front door, she spotted a piece of folded paper that had been slipped through the mail slot. The familiar shape brought a smile to her face and gave her Christmas spirit wings. A snowflake. She unfolded the paper to read the note in Colin's handwriting: *I Love You. Open the door.*

Behind the glass door stood a six-foot-four man with sandy hair. Her stomach jumped as she opened the door to reveal a grinning Colin.

"What are you doing here?"

He dropped to his knee. Palm up, he presented her with an open black velvet box. In the center was a sparkling emerald-cut diamond surrounded by rounds in the pattern of a snowflake. "Will you marry me?"

She laced her fingers and drew her hands up. She had no words for him. All she could do was skip her gaze from his glacier blues to the glint of the ring and then back.

He raised a brow and nudged the box upward. "Well?"

She giggled. "Yes. A thousand times yes."

"Em. Where do you want these boxes?"

Emma fussed over an autumn-themed table she'd set with a sample of a new line of fine china she planned to stock. Crystal wine glasses and silver flatware graced the lace tablecloth. The table setting complemented her shabby chic shop motif with a porcelain pumpkin surrounded by yellow and orange flowers as the centerpiece. Perfect.

Today she'd planned a light dinner of fresh tossed greens, croissants filled with chicken salad, wine, and cheesecake for the finale. They'd enjoy being together in the quiet shop as they ate and finalized their wedding guest list.

She picked up a box of matches. The only way to go was old school for her shabby shop. "Put them in the back room. I'll unpack tomorrow."

A thump came from behind. "Please be careful. Something might break."

"Right." Colin's footsteps approached and he reached around her from behind. His warmth caused an instant fury of butterflies to race over her body. He nuzzled her ear and whispered, "I love you, my future Mrs. Brockman."

"Oh, really? What makes you so sure I'll take your name?" She blew out the match and turned in his arms. The glow of candlelight filled the dark shop with dim light.

He smiled. He placed a tiny kiss on her forehead. "A..." One on the tip of her nose. "Man..." One adorned one corner of her mouth. "Can..." Another kiss he placed on the other corner. "Only..." He took in her lips with a long slow kiss then pulled away. "Hope."

She melted and wrapped her arms around his neck. "Mr. Brockman, you're very persuasive. How can I say no?"

He winked. "The table looks great, and Mrs. Brockman, you'll spoil me if you keep treating me like the king that I am."

She shook her head. "Really? Again, with the Mrs. Brockman." Her finger poked his chest. "I haven't decided, but you'll be the first to know when I do."

She glanced over her shoulder without releasing the man she loved. "Let's eat and go over that list."

Colin pulled out her chair then poured the wine before he sat across from her. He held up his glass. "To us and our long life together."

They clinked their glasses and she responded, "To us."

In the candlelight, she studied the man she fell in love with the first day she met him. He'd changed her life and helped her realize she wasn't alone and that she did deserve to be loved.

"Colin." She reached for his hand. "I haven't told you how much I love you, today."

His mouth inched into a full smile as he wrapped his fingers around her hand and squeezed. "I love you too, Mrs. Brockman."

A loud huff followed by a gush of air escaped her lungs. "You're not going to let this go. Mood killer." She tried to pull her hand free but he tightened his grip.

"You can call yourself anything you like as long as you love me for the rest of your life."

Her insides turned to mush. *How could she deny this man*? She covered his hand with hers. "How about a compromise? Emma Ruddeford-Brockman."

His eyes shifted to one side while he thought. "I like the sound of it." Then he gazed straight into Emma's eyes. "Mrs. Brockman," he said followed by a quick wink. He pulled her hand toward him and touched his lips to it.

"You are hopeless. But I love it." She got up and motioned for him to scooch away from the table. As soon as there was enough space, she sat on his lap and laid her head against his chest. His arms encircled her as he ran his fingers up and down her back. The steady thump of his heart and his strong arms made this the safest place in the world for her. He kissed the top of her head. "Colin."

"Yes."

She hated to leave her safe place, but they had work to do. "We have to go over the guest list and talk about the house."

"The house. When do we need to sign the papers?"

"I've got them. If we agree, we sign them and I'll get them back to the parties to be."

Emma sat up. "We can talk about the house while we eat." A peck on his cheek signaled the start of her plan as she walked back to her seat. "Give me your list of pros for the house."

Colin ran down the usual things a man wants in a home. Little yard work, a place for a man cave, a two or three-car garage, and a short distance from work.

Emma on the other hand expected lots of storage and a good kitchen layout—not that she cooked much. "I checked into the schools near the house and they all come with a good rating."

In mid-bite, he stopped. "I find it hard to see me as a father."

"Why? You'll make a great father."

"I never had one. You know, no role model."

"That doesn't matter." She laid a hand across her chest and patted. "You'll know what to do because it comes from here. You also have Rob."

"Yeah, but will I be able to handle all ten of the kids?"

Emma was in the middle of taking a sip of wine. His expectations of ten children caused her to choke as she swallowed. "Did you say ten?" He had to be nuts to think she'd agree to that many. "Colin, we talked about this. We agreed on two."

"Well, I am the newly appointed president of the Pendleton Financial Group and we can afford that many."

Could he be serious? With a squint she scrutinized him. "You're joking?

Aren't you?"

A hardy laugh filled the air. "I just wanted a reaction. I know we said two, but could we negotiate for three?"

"Let's have the first one and see how that goes. Agreed."

"Agreed."

"Now, do we sign the papers or not."

"Where's a pen?"

They finished their meal and ran through the guest list. Colin continued to make jokes the entire time. Something she loved about him.

He'd act all serious and say something that took her a few seconds to realize he'd pulled her leg, again. She'd laugh and that encouraged him to continue. But laughing was good.

Before she met Colin, she never laughed. Now, that had changed. Laughter became a part of her life and she planned many years of good times with this man.

They cleared the table and carried the dishes to the back where Colin washed as Emma reset the table as a fall display.

"Well, backroom's all done." He walked toward her with a rectangular white box he placed on the table. "I have a surprise. Open it."

Emma slid off the lid. She gasped. "They're prettier than I expected."

In her hand, she held a glacier blue wedding invitation. At the top, written in silver across a paper snowflake, their wedding date, December 24th. She caught a breath.

A snowflake was now her good luck charm. Which made her the luckiest girl in Canada. Truly, she was blessed to have such a full and satisfying life. She glanced at Colin as he studied the invitation and her heart swelled.

My love, until death do us part.

Karen Pugh was born in Chicago, Illinois, and graduated from Amundsen-Mayfair City College with an ADN in Nursing. She has had a long interest in writing. She helped create the League of Romance Writers based in Houston, Texas where she lives with her husband, two dogs, and her garden.

Currently In Print and Ebook

Shattered Fate The Belinda and Robert saga came to Linda after reminiscing about her experiences during her college years and is loosely based on those events. She approached Karen with the idea of a romance novel. Karen's experiences in nursing contributed to the theme of the plot. Combining their talents and ideas, they embarked on their first novel.

Destiny Reborn is the sequel of Belinda and Robert's life, as the two discover the reasons for their attraction.

Paper Snowflakes for Christmas continues the adventures of Colin Brockman, after his breakup with Belinda and his move to Canada in *Destiny Reborn.* This short Christmas novel is promised to delight the reader and spark romance.

Coming in 2024 In Print and Ebook

Fulling Destiny is the final chapter in the lives of Belinda and Robert as they navigate learning about each other, life, and family when the pair proves *A Happy Ever After* can be forever.

Printed in the USA
CPSIA information can be obtained
at www.ICGtesting.com
CBHW021151190724
11674CB00001B/164

9 780989 024754